WARNING

This book contains sexually explicit scenes and adult language. It may be considered offensive to some readers. This book is for sale to adults ONLY.

* * * * * * * * * * * * * * * * *

Please store your files wisely where they cannot be accessed by underage readers.

ISBN-13: 978-1987863529
ISBN-10: 1987863526

Other Books by Darla Dunbar:

<u>Romeo Alpha Blood Lines Romance Series</u> (This series follows "<u>The Romeo Alpha BBW Paranormal Shifter Romance Series</u>")

Twenty-four years have passed in relative peace for Amanda and Romeo. They've raised five children into adulthood and are thoroughly enjoying their lives as the Alpha King and Queen of the werewolves. At twenty-four, Sarina is just stepping into her powers and will be ripe for mating when her birthday comes in two weeks. What no one knows is the danger that lurks just outside their tight knit community. Romeo has made peace with the other clans and has enjoyed that peace, but it will all come crashing down around him when his oldest daughter comes of age to take a mate.

<u>The Alpha Feud BBW Paranormal Shifter Romance Series</u>

Eliza's life consisted of reporting on boring, crowd-pleasing events, like their country livestock fair. With the arrival of two handsome brothers, the lives of Eliza and her best friend, Melissa, are shaken to the core. For Eliza, the arrival of this new man becomes a test of her relationship with her current boyfriend, who she's been happily living with for over six years. Does Hayden, a complete stranger, really wield the power to make Eliza reconsider her relationship with Andrew?

<u>The Alpha Packed BBW Paranormal Shifter Romance Series</u>

Darlene has led a quiet life since suffering through a terrible break-up. She wants nothing more than to spend her time in front of the TV, away from any sort of trouble. But all that goes down the drain when handsome, rugged and rough Idris comes into her life. He is a werewolf on the lookout for his missing pack leader. Darlene quickly finds herself pulled towards this mysterious man and at the same time finds herself falling deeper and deeper into the world of the supernatural.

<u>The Daemon Paranormal Romance Chronicles</u>

The daemon infighting can only be stopped when a strong leader emerges to calm the different factions. Juno appears to be at the heart of the conflict. Things become complicated when Phoebe and Supay try to negotiate with the siren, Juno. The love triangle among Phoebe, Supay and Apollo become tense when Juno's meddling threatens to destroy any romance that develops.

<u>The Mind Talker Paranormal Romance Series</u>

Ananda finds herself on the run and she's not alone. With help from Jared, a stranger that she just met, the two evade capture by an organization that is intent on hunting her kind. Ananda and Jared are able to read minds. When an unfortunate incident happened involving a disturbed individual that resulted in the death of his schoolmates, the secret organization decided to take action.

<u>The Leather Satchel Paranormal Romance Series</u>

Valtina is stuck in Middle World, unable to pass on to The Afterlife. In order to redeem herself from past deeds done, she must help bring romance back into the world and stop The Dark Side from destroying love in its entirety. Following orders issued by Ladaya and armed with a leather satchel filled with the appropriate tools and weapons, Valtina embraces each mission with enthusiasm.

Get the latest update on new releases from the author at:

https://darladunbar.com/newsletter/

This book is Part One of the "The Romeo Alpha BBW Paranormal Shifter Romance Series"

Book 1

Amanda Walker thinks that she has a normal and boring life. That is until after her 24th birthday. Everything changes when she meets the man who says he is supposed to be her husband. Denying everything the man says, she fights him every step of the way. But after he kidnaps her, Amanda discovers that there are some things about her family that her parents kept a secret all these years. Among the history of the family, she learns secrets she thought only happened in story books. Can Amanda tell the difference between truth and lies or does she hold the key to a mysterious legacy?

Book 2

After finally finding out who she really is, Amanda is ecstatic with her new life. Everything, however, is about to change. When a fire breaks out among the wolves, all suspicion is pointed towards her brother. Being forced to make the biggest choice of her life, Amanda must decide if being with Romeo is really where she should be or if her destiny lies elsewhere. Will she take the plunge that her heart is pushing her towards or will she do what is expected of her? Time can only tell.

Book 3

Now that Amanda is separated from her new husband and the other Radiants, she must go on a journey to discover the power inside of her to defeat her evil brother, Dean. She discovers the deep rooted history of her kind as the lines between good and evil blur when her sister-in-law begins to fall for the enemy. To compound the situation, there is a surprise pregnancy that is endangered from the escalating conflict between Amanda and her brother.

Book 4

Coming off the death of her evil brother, Amanda still feels anxious. She feels that the Radiants should stick around in case Lilith decides to make an appearance. When a woman shows up claiming to know Penelope as well as Amanda's family, it seems almost too good to be true. The spirit of Amanda's aunt shows up with a warning that confirms her suspicions. The new guest has a deadly secret that will lead to devastating consequences. Will Amanda get her happy ending, or will she lose the family she has worked so hard to build?

A BBW Paranormal Shifter Romance Series

Romeo Alpha

Book One

By Darla Dunbar

Copyright Revelry Publishing 2015

Table of Contents

Chapter One

AMANDA WONDERED how the hell she had gotten so far away from home. When she walked, she usually didn't go past a couple of blocks, but she felt so different today. Something was pushing her further and in a different direction, and she wasn't sure what it was. But she didn't care at the moment, because she just wanted to walk.

Not thinking twice about where she was going, she let her gut instinct give her the direction she needed.

Her grandmother had always told her to go with her gut. She'd said human instinct was better than anything. "Intuition is a girl's best friend," she would say, and then they would both laugh. Talks she and her grandmother had always seemed to pop into her head at the strangest of times, like now.

Here she was, going for a walk, and wondering why she wanted to go in a different direction, and there was her grandmother's voice in her head, propelling her along. Amanda missed her grandmother more with every passing year.

Amanda paused and thought about her life thus far. She had just graduated from college and started working in the local animal hospital, but it wasn't quite like she had thought. She didn't see the care and passion she'd hoped to find in the industry. In the city, being a vet was all about how much money you could make, how many pets you could treat. And, at twenty-four, it was hard to be taken seriously.

Her two female roommates were nice, but they all just went their separate ways. They didn't eat ice cream and watch movies like on *Friends*. They didn't share secrets or even laugh or hang out. They really just slept in the same apartment, and they usually weren't even home at the same time. Except Amanda, that is.

Amanda was always at home, it seemed. She had nowhere else to go, really. The other two girls spent most nights out with their real friends or their boyfriends. Amanda lived a lonely life, but she was happy. At least, she was pretty sure she was happy. After all, she had an upstanding career, and she still had money left over from her savings.

Both her parents had been killed in a car accident years ago. Amanda had graduated from high school with no family there that day or on the day she graduated from college. It was what it was, though, and she knew that her parents watched her from Heaven.

The only positive thing was that her parents had been prepared and had made sure they left enough money and a big enough life insurance policy to help her out. They would be surprised but happy knowing how much that money had helped her in the years after their death. She was proud to say that she was able to live off of it through her college years. She'd never even had to get a job like most kids did. Amanda had been able to focus on her classes.

That freedom wasn't worth it, though. She would have worked three jobs at a time while going to school for one more day with her parents.

However, the account was finally starting to dry up, and she needed to think about what she would do. Sure, she had a new job that could pay her bills, but those loans were piling up with interest. Even a vet job only went so far.

Amanda sighed as she began the trek back toward the house.

Amanda liked her walks in the evening. It helped her to relax, enjoying the quiet time alone. And while Amanda wasn't overweight by any means, it helped slim her waistline, which showed those extra biscuits she liked every now and again.

She turned and began to make her way back to the townhouse she shared with her roommates, but stopped as she heard a noise.

A rustling came from behind her, and she turned to see the bushes shaking. Looking over to the other side of the sidewalk, she saw those bushes shake as well. Not wanting to wait around to find out what was behind the leaves, she took off at a run. She swore she heard a growl come from behind her, but she didn't turn to see what was chasing her. That would only slow her down. As she reached the door to her home, she quickly turned the knob and went through headfirst. Shutting the door quickly, she looked out the window. She got a glimpse of a long black furry tail as something ran around to the side of her building.

"What in the world are you doing, Amanda?" Betsy stood there looking at her inquisitively.

"Something was chasing me."

"What?"

"I don't know what it was, but something big and furry was chasing me. I saw a long black tail just now when I walked into the house."

"You mean when you dove into the house?" Betsy's grin faded. "I'll call the game warden. If there is a big animal outside, then none of us need to go out there until they find it and get rid of it."

"Well, I don't want them to kill it."

"I know, silly, but if it's a wild animal, they can take it out to the National Forest and let it loose. The city is no place for a wild animal." Betsy turned and picked up the phone from the receiver.

Amanda stood in shocked silence as she listened to her roommate tell the person on the other end of the phone what had happened.

She knew from Betsy's tone that she and the person on the other end of the phone were questioning her sanity. They lived in a big city, and the closest thing they got to a wild animal was a stray cat or two. They didn't even get raccoons. If there was some huge animal like she thought, then it would make headline news.

Shaking her head in aggravation, Amanda turned toward her room. She suddenly felt silly and didn't want to have to explain what she saw to any more people.

"Amanda? Where are you going? They are on their way and might need to talk to you."

"Tell them it was a dog. Now that I'm thinking about it, it kind of looked like that couple that lives down the road's greyhound. Maybe he just got out."

"Are you sure, Amanda?" Betsy asked, turning and saying something into the phone.

Without saying another word, Amanda shut the door to her room tight and then quickly locked the door. She looked over her room and, seeing the window open and the curtains blowing in the breeze, she ran over to push the window pane down and lock it tight. As she stood there, she looked out into the woods that made up her backyard. There, in the distance, two yellow eyes stared back at her.

Suddenly, more eyes appeared, and it seemed the animals went on forever. She was amazed, since the woods behind her house were very dense and small. The dark night was lit with a full moon. A shiver raced through her as she stood there and stared into the first set of yellow eyes. She quickly shut the curtains and went to sit on her bed. She didn't think she would ever be able to fall asleep knowing what was out there. As she laid her head on the pillow, her mind wondered to large beasts with yellow eyes and sharp fangs. But she was soon fast asleep.

<<◇>>

Amanda awoke with a yawn. It had been almost a month since the incident with what she now called a dog. She had agreed with Betsy that her mind had been playing tricks on her that night. There were often times when she was sure she felt eyes on her, and she would turn in one direction or another, looking. What she was seeking, she didn't know, but somewhere in the back of her mind, she just wanted to know if the eyes she had seen that night had been real or just part of her dreams that evening. She was still so uneasy about it that her walks seemed to get earlier and earlier each evening.

She was just about to walk out the door when her phone started ringing. She quickly grabbed it and pushed the button to answer it.

"Hello."

"Ms. Walker?"

"Yes?"

"Hello, Ms. Walker, my name is Ernest Montgomery. I am calling to tell you that your aunt has passed away."

"My aunt? But I don't have any family. You must have the wrong Ms. Walker."

"No, ma'am. Your father was Joshua Walker, correct? Mother Maureen Walker?"

"Yes."

"Then, I have the right Ms. Walker. It is your father's sister I am referring to. She unexpectedly passed away from a heart attack. I am very sorry for your loss."

"Oh, my gosh! I never knew I even had any family. I am very sad that I didn't get to meet her."

"Yes, ma'am. I'm sure. She was a nice woman. I have also called you to see if you can meet with me. I need to go over her will with you."

"Her will?"

"Yes, ma'am. Your aunt was a wealthy woman."

"Oh? Um, okay. When would you like to meet?"

"The sooner, the better."

"Okay. How about today?"

"That would be great. I am in Slatesville, in the valley. "

"Oh. Okay. That is just forty-five minutes from me. I can be there in a couple of hours."

"Sounds good, ma'am. I am at the *Montgomery Law Firm*. I am the only attorney in the town."

"Okay. Thank you, sir. I will see you soon."

"Yes, ma'am. I'll be waiting."

Amanda fell back on the couch, stunned, for what seemed like forever. Everything was pushed to the back of her mind as she thought about what she had just learned. She had a family. Well, she *did* have a family. Now her aunt was gone. Could there be others in her family who she knew nothing about? She didn't know, but she did know one thing. She wasn't going to find out sitting around here, twiddling her thumbs. She needed to get going fast.

Amanda headed for the kitchen. She wasn't surprised to see that no one was there. Of course her roommates weren't home. They were either in class or with their boyfriends.

Smiling, she made a cup of coffee and drank it slowly, thinking about what she might find out. Then, with a deep sigh, she made her way to her car. She looked at the small Honda with pride. It was a pile of junk to some, but it held a special place in her heart. She hadn't been able to get rid of her father's car. Instead, she had sold her own.

She looked down at the small picture he had taped to the dash near the speedometer. She was about six in the picture, and she had been holding her mom's cheeks in her hands as she kissed her.

She remembered the day like it was yesterday. They had just got to a cabin they vacationed in. She had enjoyed herself so much. The little cabin had one bedroom with a queen-sized bed where her parents slept and a set of bunk beds for her. They had stayed up late roasting marshmallows as her father told her scary stories about wolves and vampires. She had ended up in their bed, snuggled between the two of them. They had spent the next day hiking and walking trails and seeing tons of waterfalls and animals.

She had loved it and had never forgotten. It soon became a family tradition to go camping every year. After some of those trips, they didn't return home. Instead, they moved on to a different location. The constant moving had been hard on her as a kid, but she would have never told her parents that. She had felt like they were hiding something from her. Of course, she had been young back then and had blown it off as childhood curiosity. Now, with this new family member, she wasn't so sure.

Her parents had been very quiet people. They seemed cautious of everything going on around them and were even a little jumpy at times. Maybe there was more going on here than she thought. She needed to find out.

She wiped away a tear and go in the car. The car had a huge dent in one side and was almost fifteen years old, but it got her where she needed to go. She slid the car into drive and smiled to herself.

"Dad would be proud that his car was still running so good, wouldn't he, Trixy?" She and her father had named the car together.

Amanda turned onto the next road and made her way down the narrow two-lane road that led into the mountains. She had never been this way because her parents always went the long way around the mountains. They said they liked to take the scenic route.

She came to a small wooden sign that said *Slatesville—Welcome to your home away from home*. She smiled at the welcoming sign and kept on her way to the town. As she drove, she was amazed at how beautiful everything was. The low-hanging branches of the trees scraped the roof of the car every once in a while.

She was amazed at how many animals she saw. Deer acted as if they weren't afraid of her car. Raccoons were plentiful, and she jumped when a large black snake slithered across the road. There were people all around, and they watched her car curiously as she made her way down the street.

The town reminded her of a long lost western ghost town. It was a little spooky, and she caught herself checking the doors to make sure they were locked. The men nodded at her as she moved forward and many of the people smiled, although they held themselves back a little.

Amanda finally saw the sign that said *Montgomery Law Firm*. She pulled into one of the many vacant parking spots and slowly got out of the car. A handsome man leaned against the building she was about to enter. His brown eyes had flecks of yellow and orange in their deep depths. She smiled slightly, and the man just continued to stare as he looked her over slowly.

"Can I help you, ma'am?"

"I am just here to see Mr. Montgomery."

"Well, you're in the right place, Miss…?"

"Oh, Amanda. Amanda Walker. And you are?"

Something changed in his eyes as he smiled at her and made his way to her side. He held out his hand to her. "Name's Curtis Livingston."

"Oh. Do you live here?"

"Yes. I'm one of the controlling partners here in Slatesville. Well, I have to be going. It was good to meet you."

"You, too, Mr. Livingston."

"Please, call me Curt. Everyone does."

"Only if you call me Amanda."

"That's a deal, sweet lady." She flushed all over when he raised her hand to his lips and gently caressed her knuckles with a brief touch of his mouth. She felt the rise in temperature in her cheeks spread across her upper chest. She stood there and watched as he walked away from her down the street to slip inside a store. She felt foolish and realized that she had been staring. She shook her head, trying to think straight and clear the thoughts that were running through her mind.

Amanda was always aware that she wasn't the Barbie doll type of girl. Although she wasn't fat, she wasn't rail thin, which most men liked, either. Her waist and stomach didn't look like a washboard, although it didn't look like a bunch of bread dough either.

She instantly felt inadequate and quickly turned around to walk to the door of the attorney's office. Knocking, she was surprised when the door instantly opened. The man who opened the door wasn't what she expected. Mr. Montgomery was a short, pudgy man. He didn't wear a business suit, and he didn't seem stuffy at all. He was older and had a short goatee around his mouth. His hair was pulled back into a ponytail at the back of his neck, and he smiled when he saw her.

"You must be Amanda. You look just like your father, except for your eyes. You have your mother's eyes. Let's hope you didn't inherit your father's temper, though," he chuckled.

"You knew my father?"

"Oh, why yes, my dear. We grew up together, Josh and I. Have to say we got into a lot of trouble as kids, and your aunt Mabel was always there to wag her finger and tell on us. You see, there were the three of us; Joshua, Jeremiah, and I. We were called the three musketeers. Mabel wanted to be the fourth, but you know boys. We would never let her, so she always ran and told on us to get back at us for not including her; the little minx." He told the story fondly, and she instantly knew that this man held her family in the highest regard. She also knew he was her ticket to finding out the truth about her family.

"Do I have any more family that I don't know of?" She held her breath, as though she were a child again, asking if Santa Claus was real.

"I am sure you do, my dear. Unfortunately, your aunt was the last of your father's line. She couldn't have any children, and most of the family was killed in a fire in '90. I am sure there is still family on your mother's side, though. However, I must warn you that they are not the kind of people you want to know. Now, if you will come in, I will tell you about everything that now belongs to you."

"What?"

"Oh, my dear, you must know that your father's family had a legacy. You are the only Traverse left to take over the family business."

"What? I don't know what you're talking about."

"They never did tell you who you really are, did they? Oh, you poor child. I am afraid you are going to learn some things about yourself that are going to be hard for you. You must still be a virgin as well."

"I beg your pardon, sir, but I don't see how that's any of your damn business."

"No, my dear, I do not mean to be crude. I was just saying that you have never undergone the Change. It will happen, though. You recently turned twenty-four, and everything changes now."

"What change? What in the hell are you talking about?"

"They hid that from you, too? Oh my gosh. You don't know? Oh, Lord. Okay, first things first. You are now the owner of your family's estate."

"Family estate? So I have a house."

He smiled kindly at her. "Not just a house, my dear. It is what holds the legacy of your family name together. The estate has fifteen bedrooms with their own bathrooms and fireplaces, a kitchen, dining room, parlor, living area, office, library, Carolina room, staff quarters, wrap-around porch with two different sections screened in, pool, tennis courts and 300 acres. It was the pride and joy of your ancestor, Edgar. He was a distant grandfather of yours."

"Oh my gosh."

"Yes, ma'am. How about this? How about I get the keys and directions to the place? You go take a look at it, and then we can talk tomorrow about what you want to do. Stephan has been looking over things, and since your aunt's death, he has given everyone time off until you arrive and decide where to go from there."

Amanda wasn't sure she had the energy to deal with all of this tonight. "Unfortunately, it is very late. Is there somewhere that I can stay for a couple days and then I can go from there and take the day tomorrow to go look at the place?"

"That is perfect. Just give me a second, and I'll find a place for you to stay tonight."

Amanda sat quietly and listened to him talk on his phone. She didn't even hear his words as she thought of what she was going to do.

"I have gotten you a little cabin to rent down the road," he said, drawing her attention back to him. "It is in the woods a little but has electricity and such. On such short notice, I couldn't find anything else. It is only about ten minutes away. The key will be under the mat at the front door. Just go on in and make yourself at home."

"That is perfect. Thank you so much."

"You're welcome, my dear, and we will talk tomorrow. Say ten o'clock tomorrow morning? We will meet here and go to see the house together."

"Perfect. Thank you, Mr. Montgomery."

Chapter Two

As she made her way out to her car, she felt something strange build inside her. What was going on? She had just found out in the last hour that she had family she knew nothing about, and she'd inherited a huge estate. Her luck was finally turning up, and she whistled as she made her way to the car. Hopping in, she turned the radio off and made a U-turn in the parking lot before pulling off in the other direction. She couldn't help but smile as she thought of what was happening.

Her thoughts took a path of their own as she drove down the one-lane road ahead. What should she do? Should she stay in this little town? What about her career? She couldn't see spending her life laid up with a drink in her hand doing nothing. That just wasn't the kind of person Amanda was.

The town was small, and she didn't even know if they needed a veterinarian. What would she do if they didn't? She brushed off the questions that bombarded her head and ran through her mind at a million miles a second. She would have to think about it tomorrow. Then, she might be able to think straight. Right now, she needed to just get over the shock of everything she had been told. She needed to find out just who she was, and the estate was the best place to start looking into it.

On the road up ahead, she saw a disturbance but couldn't make out if animals or humans were causing the problem. She could have sworn that she saw a tail or two swinging in the air like some kind of dog fight. Leaning forward, she applied pressure to the middle of her steering wheel, honking her horn loudly a couple of times. They all seemed to scatter into the surrounding woods.

She began looking frantically around in the woods around her. Something wasn't right. It was the same feeling she had gotten back home before she had gotten chased by the creature with yellow eyes.

She should be coming up to the driveway of the cabin. If it wasn't for the wooden sign that said *Timber Wolf Lodge*, she would have driven right past it. There were no street signs anywhere, and all the roads had turned into dirt roads a while back. She pulled up to a little one-floor stone cabin, and saw with relief that the porch light had been left on for her.

She got out, grabbed her bag, and walked to the door. The air around went silent. Something was going on. Maybe she just wasn't used to the quiet, or maybe it was too quiet. Shouldn't the crickets be chirping or some frogs croaking into the night? It was as if someone had pushed mute, except there wasn't even the static that came from the television.

Something made her turn around. It was her gut feeling again, and she quickly bent down. Her hand fumbled under the mat, but there was nothing there. She was frantic now as she looked around in the growing dark.

Suddenly, she heard a rustling in the bushes behind her. Then it happened again on the other side. Her fingers went numb, and she ran her hands over the porch flooring hurriedly. Unexpectedly, the front door jerked open, and she was hauled across the threshold by the front of her shirt. She screamed as loud as she could, but she knew there wasn't anyone nearby.

Why didn't she get her pepper spray out? Well, probably because she had been more scared of the four-legged monsters in the woods and not the two-legged ones. As the door slammed shut, she spun around in time to connect her little right fist with the chest in front of her. Her father had taught her early on how to defend herself in a situation like this. She had to breathe and think straight under pressure in order to accomplish what she wanted to do, and that was to get the hell away from whoever was now holding her.

"Who the hell are you? And what the hell do you think you are doing?" she seethed as she slowly raised her head and threw silent sparks at the bright blue eyes meeting her own with amusement. Her eyes climbed up the wide expanse of chest enclosed in a flannel shirt that would have been impressive if she wasn't so pissed off. He had the sleeves rolled up to his elbows and the top three buttons were missing, showing an even more impressive display. She was shaking with rage, shock, and fear.

"Saving you," came his deep but simple reply.

Amanda walked into the next room and came to an abrupt stop. The man standing there was not the man who had been there before. This man had long brown hair and a smile on his face. He must have heard her in the other room, trying to open the windows and throwing the chair.

"What? Is my door open to everyone? I really need to find somewhere else to stay. Who are you?" she asked with exasperation.

"My name is Joseph. Younger brother to Romeo. You will meet the others shortly," he said with a bow.

"Others? You mean there are more of you?" Amanda looked at him with a heavy frown. How many more would walk into her door?

"Yes. Five brothers and two sisters. There is Romeo, the oldest, who you have already met, Sebastian, Elijah, myself, Bryce, and the twins; Aurora and Audri. We are a dedicated group."

"My goodness, I guess I will have the pleasure of meeting everyone," she scoffed. This man had a carefree humor to him that the brooding Romeo did not share.

"Yes, there are a total of 214 wolves," he said.

"Wolves?" What in the hell was he talking about?

"*Joseph!* You can go. Tell Audri to give us some time. I have to explain things now," Romeo interrupted loudly.

Amanda turned and looked at him. He stood there with his hands on his hips. He wore low-slung, light-colored jeans and a black T-shirt that fit snug across his large biceps. She had to admit he was an excellent specimen if she ever saw one.

What was she thinking? This man broke into her rental and was pretty much holding her hostage. As Joseph slunk out the door with a broad smile, she turned to look into the bluest eyes she had ever seen. Romeo had an annoyed expression as he stared at his brother. What an ass!

"Can I leave now?" she asked rudely.

"No. Sit. We need to talk," he said a little more sternly than necessary.

"No, I will stand. It will make it easier to leave that way." She crossed her arms over her chest.

Romeo heaved a long sigh before grabbing her by the arm to push her down on the couch. Electricity sizzled up her arm where his hand had touched. He must have felt it too, because he looked at her warily. He sat beside her. She quickly rose but sat back down at his next words.

"We will start with your parents." He must have known it would get her attention.

"What do you know about my parents?" This man she had never seen in her life was talking about her parents. Had she walked into the *Twilight Zone*? First, there was all this about an inheritance, and now, this man was talking about her parents? What was going on?

"Your parents were part of our pack," he stated with a shrug.

"How do you know who I am, and how did you know my parents?" She could feel the panic welling up inside of her. First, she found out that she had family she didn't even know about and an estate was left to her. Now, this man was saying that he knew her family. Or at least, knew of them, and that they were from this small town she'd never been to.

She thought about it and knew instinctively that it made sense. That would explain why her parents never went through the mountains. But, wolves, really? Come on. Did she look dumb or something?

"First, let's start with me telling you that you are in danger and cannot go anywhere without me or one of my brothers. Others will find you, and you will not like the consequences." He sounded serious.

"What do you mean, the consequences? Just what the hell is this? Look, I have been on my own since I was seventeen. I don't need your help or your guidance or whatever the hell you are trying to do. I want to leave!" she cried desperately, feeling trapped. Was she ever going to wake up from this strange nightmare?

"Let me tell you the story, and then we will decide what to do after," he said sternly as he patted the seat beside him. She knew he was getting angry, but she didn't give a rat's ass. She was fuming. What gave him the right to keep her prisoner?

"Fine," she said as she sat stiffly beside him.

"Many centuries ago, a man by the name of Fenris was living in the Carpathian Mountains. Some legends say he contracted a virus. Other legends say that God himself made him the way he became."

"What did he become?" she asked hesitantly.

"Fenris had two forms; one man and one wolf. On full moons, his body would change into that of the wolf for the night until the sun rose back over the sky. He met a woman by the name of Lilith. The two fell in love and soon he told her of his secret. Their male children also took on the gene to transform at the age of eighteen, but their daughters did not. This continued until centuries later, when one of the women of the line and one of the men from the line mated. This produced a new line. Not only could the men transform, but so could the women. The line has lived on, and we are the current generation." He sat back and let her take it in.

"Okay, let me get this straight. You are saying that you and your family are from this line and can turn into wolves on a full moon? Really, come on, do I look dumb?" She stood up, ready to get out of there.

"No, it isn't just us. It's you as well. Now, sit, so I can tell you about your parents." He remained firm.

Amanda looked at him like he had grown two heads. "What if I just try to leave? What will you do then?" She stood with her hands on her hips, mirroring his attitude earlier.

"I will stop you, and if you do figure out a way to leave, I will find you and bring you back," he replied simply with a smile. "Your parents were part of the community as well, Amanda. Now, please sit." He waved his arm.

"My parents?" She looked at Romeo with wonder as she realized that he was being completely serious. Either he was really clinically insane, or she was dreaming. This was the stuff nightmares were made of. It wasn't real. It couldn't be.

"Yes, if a wolf male beds a wolf female, their children transform. But if a wolf male beds a human woman, then the male children Change, but the female children become breeders only. Your father was a male wolf, and your mother was a human."

"You mean I am a breeder? So what is my job; to lie on my back and sleep with every wolf man? Have you lost your damn mind?" It was becoming too much for her to handle. If she pinched herself, would she wake up in her own bed?

"On the contrary; nobody will be sharing your bed, Amanda, but *me*."

Determination lined his face. This man really was crazy.

"So I am in danger from the crazy-ass man sitting beside me." She rose quickly and turned to leave, but she didn't get far. Suddenly, he was in front of her, his arms were wrapped around her waist and he had pulled her to him. If it wasn't for her hands on his chest to keep her distance, they would have been flush against each other.

She could feel the steady beat of his heart under her right hand and looked up into his face, fuming. "What will you do; force yourself on me?"

"There will be no forcing. You will come to me of your own will. That, I can promise you." His eyes held many meanings as he stared down at her.

"So, you are the one I must run from then." Her breathing was rapid and shallow as she tried to catch her breath. For some reason, it had become increasingly hard to breath around him.

"No, there are others who have found you, and believe me; they would have no problem tossing you from one to the other till you were with child. Our community cherishes our women, we don't abuse them. You could be in worse hands. Also, since your father was part of a royal blood line in another community, you will be with the alpha of ours. *Me!*" He spoke the last part like a roar.

Yes, she could see him as the alpha; captain of the football team, star athlete and royal pain in the ass. She had to get away. But first, she was curious. "How do you know who I am, and how do you know I am part werewolf?"

He grinned. "We have been watching you since your parents' death. Your father was a good friend of my father, and he entrusted your welfare to him. Second, I know you are part werewolf because I can smell you."

She didn't have time to think before his lips descended to hers. His lips were soft and warm. His hands squeezed her waist. At her gasp, he took the advantage and slipped his tongue inside her mouth.

He explored the recesses of her mouth, and she couldn't help the groan as he pulled her even closer. Her arms wrapped around his neck on their own, and soon she was kissing him back. His hands ran up and down her back to slowly curve under her ass. He hoisted her up against him, and she felt his hardness against her pelvic bone.

Suddenly, a loud knock sounded at the door. He pulled his lips away and looked down at her as he sat her back on the floor. "We will finish this later," he said with promise in his eyes.

She felt the blush spread from her face down her chest. "That will never happen again," she said as she stepped back.

He just grinned at her and turned to open the door. "We will see, little one."

She had barely contained her composure before two girls walked into the room. They were about eighteen and gorgeous. Both wore radiant smiles. She could tell by the look of love that he sent their way that these must be the youngest two members of the family; the twins Aurora and Audri.

The light-haired girl rushed to her, bubbling with excitement. The dark-haired girl slowly followed her. "Oh, finally we get a sister. I am so excited. You will love the family and Romeo, even though he is a little overbearing sometimes."

"Yeah, and he is way too overprotective. You know, I have to take someone with me to sit outside when I go to college. It's so annoying like we can't take care of ourselves," the dark-haired one complained.

Romeo shook his head. "It's for your own good. Now help her get settled in. I'm going to go check the guard. None of you go anywhere until I return. Understood? Joseph will be back shortly." He walked through the door without waiting for their response.

Amanda opened the door to see if she could get away, and he turned to look straight at her with a stern look. Suddenly, the other brother was beside him. She turned around and slammed the door with frustration. He had to be the most cocky and arrogant man she had ever met. She turned to see both women looking at her with sadness in their eyes.

"Come," the dark-haired one offered. "We will help you and fix some tea."

She walked toward the twins and realized she hadn't gone to the store yet, so there was no tea. They walked into the little kitchen, and she instructed them to take a seat at the little round table.

As she opened cabinets and the refrigerator, she noticed it was already stocked full. As the dark-haired one put on a tea kettle with water and pulled pastries from the cabinet, the light-haired one sat down across from Amanda.

"My name is Aurora, and this is my twin sister, Audri." Aurora had light brown hair that reached down her back almost to her waist in little ringlets. She had light blue eyes like Romeo and dimples. You could tell she was the talkative and bubbly one of the two.

Audri had dark brown, almost black hair, which lay straight as an arrow down her back to her waist. Her eyes were dark blue. She had sharper features and seemed to be more cautious than her sister. She also looked like the one to take control. They both stood about her height with petite figures and features.

Audri handed Amanda a cup and set one down in front of her sister. She went back to the counter to pick up her own and came to sit on the other side. They sat in silence for little bit.

Amanda finally started asking questions. She wanted to know everything. If what Romeo said was true, then her whole world had just turned upside down. Everything she'd believed her whole life was a lie.

She found out that her father had made a trip to the mountains the night her parents were killed. Her father had spoken to Jeremiah, the twins' father, that day, telling him about Amanda and everything that had been going on in their lives. That was the day her fate and life were sealed. Why, she didn't know, but the two older men pledged the marriage between her and Romeo.

Audri stated that their father had kept watch over her through college and always watched her, no matter where she was or what she was doing. They had to wait until she turned twenty-four, which was the age that a breeder would come into full bloom. Amanda had just turned twenty-four a week ago.

"I can't believe that people have watched me for so long and none of you ever told me about my family. What about my aunt? Did she not care enough to tell me who she was? Did she even come to my father's funeral?"

"Look, your aunt was a good woman," Audri snapped. "She mourned the loss of your father from her life not once, but twice. The first was when he ran, and the second time was in his death. You cannot imagine what she went through to keep the other packs from your father and mother. Unfortunately, she gave her life in that battle, and due to that, our community has lost a good woman who stood for values and honor."

Aurora reached over and squeezed Amanda's hand. "I understand it is a lot to take in, and I understand that Romeo can be a little dominating, but maybe you should think about the full picture. Do you understand the dangers that she faced for your family, and what my father and our family are now facing to abide by your father's wishes?

"Your father was a good man and an important one," Audri continued, standing up and fairly quivering with anger. "The others know this. There are some who may just want to breed you for his bloodline. There are others who would torture and kill you just because he was an enemy. To kill off one's bloodline is the ultimate revenge. Many would have no problem screwing you and tossing you to the next wolf. My brother is not like that and forbids any of his brothers and the men in the community to even touch you. You will be his wife and bear his children. If not for your own good and welfare, then do it for the memory of your father and aunt and for the safety of my family." Audri stormed out the front door, almost colliding with Joseph on the way.

The smile on Joseph's face died as he looked at her angry features and Amanda's shell-shocked ones.

"Oh heavens, Audri, what did you say now, you little minx?"

"I told her the truth, since everyone else around here wants to walk on egg shells, including father and Romeo." Audri turned and stalked away.

Amanda tried to register everything Audri had just told her.

Aurora squeezed her hand again. "I know it is hard to take in all at once. But she is right. Your father was a very good man, and we would be proud to have you in the family. But it has to be your choice. Although, he is brooding sometimes, Romeo is a very good and honorable man. And I have heard that he's not too bad in the sack either." She grinned, playfully.

"Oh, Lord. I'm not sitting here listening to you two talk about sex. Romeo would skin me alive. I will be on the porch if you need me." Joseph scrunched up his face and left.

They both laughed outright, and for the first time since beginning the strange adventure, Amanda felt at ease.

"But I don't even know him. How do I pledge to spend the rest of my life with him?" Amanda asked in confusion.

"You will learn to know him. You will also learn our ways and my sister and I will teach you everything there is to know. Also, my father is quite anxious to meet the daughter of his best friend. Although, he has watched you in the distance and talked to you a few times, you would not even know it was him. He will come to see you tomorrow morning. Tonight will be a big night for you."

"Tonight! You mean this is to happen tonight? What if I can't? What if I don't want to?" Amanda asked, standing.

"Then, you will still be able to be taken by the other communities, and if they succeed in taking you away, then there is nothing my brother or my family can do. Once you are married, you are untouchable. Although, there are rebel groups who would still try to kidnap you, the majority of the communities will back off. It is for your safety that this must happen before the new moon."

"How do I know that what you say is the truth? This could just be a ruse." Amanda wanted reassurance of some kind, although she knew deep down what the young girl said to her was actually nothing but the truth.

"You will share each other's bed tonight, but you will not be married until after the new moon, when you can see for yourself the members of the community who can turn to their other form. This will give you the proof you need."

It sounded simple enough, but was her fate really so sealed?

"Then, why must we sleep together tonight?"

"It is Romeo's wish to have you conceive as quickly as possible. Even if you are not married but you carry another wolf's child, then you are also untouchable. But as soon as you deliver, you are free game again, unless you are married," Aurora explained.

"I think I am going to go take a shower and lay down. It has been a long day." Amanda needed to be alone and think. What in the world was her life turning into? She thought of Romeo and instantly felt warm all over. Although he was an overbearing pain in the ass, she had to admit that she was extremely attracted to him. He had the body of a god, and she instantly thought of herself. She felt frumpy compared to the two younger women, who had bodies that men would drool over with just a glance. She just couldn't get naked with Romeo. She wasn't alpha material.

"Yes. I know you are very tired, dear. You go get some sleep and we will talk some more again later." Audri rose, taking both cups to the sink. "And I am glad you are going to be my sister, Amanda. I have heard great things about you and know we will become fast friends." She smiled as she walked out the front door.

Chapter Three

Amanda walked into the large bedroom and rummaged through her things until she found a purple pajama set of shorts and a tank top. She laid them with underwear on the bed and shut the bedroom door before she went into the bathroom. She turned on the tap and checked the temperature before turning the shower on. She quickly removed her clothes, knowing she would feel much better once she got under the water.

She felt the spray of water down her back and relaxed. What was she going to do? Could she go through with this? What would happen if she didn't? She still had so many questions. She quickly rinsed and washed her hair. Soaping up the rag that she had found hanging on the bar, she ran it over her body and sighed with pleasure at the feel of the suds cleaning her skin. It was funny how a simple shower made her feel like a different person.

She turned the knob to shut the water off and grabbed a towel on the rack right outside the shower door. Quickly drying off, she wrapped the towel around her and walked into the bedroom.

She stopped short when she saw Romeo sitting on the bed. His back was propped up against the headboard, and his legs were stretched out in front of him. His eyes traveled the length of her body, and she realized she stood there in nothing but a towel. He looked as if he would devour her right then and there, a hunter on the prowl for his next meal. She knew she was that next appetizing morsel he was looking for. She wouldn't be surprised if his tongue lapped at his lips and gums in anticipation.

"What are you doing in here?" she asked breathlessly.

"Waiting for you." He stood and started to stalk toward her like an animal seeking his prey. His eyes were smoldering as they once again perused her body from head to toe. He stood in front of her and pulled her to him. She gasped as he wrapped his left arm around her slightly rounded waist and dug his other hand in her hair to pull her lips to his and all thoughts fled from her mind. She should be fighting him. Screaming, biting and scratching to get away from him. Instead she met his kiss head on.

He gave a low rumbling groan as he gripped her closer. He pulled her head back to place little kisses along her throat and took a little nip where her neck met her shoulder. Somehow, she felt the bed behind her knees, and he lifted her to place her on her back. She was amazed he could lift her so easily. He didn't even grunt or show that it took any exertion to lift her, and she suddenly felt a little better. That was until she thought of him looking at her naked. She couldn't even think of how embarrassing that was going to be.

All thoughts left her again when she felt the pressure of his weight as he followed her down to lay half on her and half beside her. His tongue stroked the shell of her ear, and her head was suddenly spinning out of control. She felt light-headed and dizzy.

"My, little one, you smell good. I cannot wait to enjoy all of you," he confessed in a low murmur. Was he for real? Did he get a good look at her, or was he partially blind? She was far from little.

His left hand gently squeezed her left breast. She looked down to see that the towel had fallen open to reveal everything to his gaze. He bent his head to take her nipple in his mouth, and she moaned at the sensation.

He chuckled. "You are very responsive. How does it make you feel?" His other hand traveled along her ribcage and across her stomach to rest on her abdomen. His hand was warm and wonderful, and she couldn't help but love the way it felt. He gently drew small circles on her skin while he moved his mouth to her other breast. His hand dipped even further to slide in her center and applied pressure on her clit. Her head swarmed with the hundreds of sensations. She had never felt anything like this before.

His lips came back up to meet hers as his hands worked over her body. There wasn't an inch of skin that he didn't touch and caress.

She couldn't help the moans that escaped her throat. One of his hands was lightly pinching and pulling her nipples into hard peaks, while the other slowly slipped a finger inside her.

She couldn't think straight, so she threw all caution to the wind and just felt. Everything in her life had been boring up until this. Everything had revolved around school and planning the future. For this one moment, she just wanted to think about how good it felt. She didn't want to think about the consequences or what she was going to do next. She just wanted to feel the sensations he caused her body to have.

She opened her mouth on a gentle sigh and met his tongue with her own. He slowly slid two fingers inside her and set a rhythm, slowly at first, then building up speed. They were both panting at this point, and she wrapped her hands around his neck. She entwined one in his soft hair and the other started its own perusal of his body. Two could play this game of sensuality, and she wondered if she could cause him to feel the same crazy pleasure he was causing to take root inside of her.

She slowly slid her hands over his biceps and across his shoulders to meet in the middle of his back. He had an amazing body, and she couldn't help but run her fingertips over the ridges of his muscles. Pressure built up inside her, and she couldn't think straight as his thumb applied pressure to her clit again while the two fingers kept a steady rhythm moving inside her. Suddenly, her back left the bed in an arch, and he took her nipple into his mouth at the same time she exploded with a loud yell.

She looked up at him, amazed, as she fell back. He watched her with a heated gaze and a grin. Heat rose in her face and spread across her chest. He chuckled as he rose up and held out his hand. She took his hand and wrapped the towel back around her. He led her to the door of the bathroom.

"Clean up and get some rest. We will have time for fun later." He leaned down and gently kissed her lips before walking away. Amanda quickly took another shower and put on the pajamas she had laid out earlier and snuggled up into bed.

She awoke sometime later to see the sun shining in through the blinds. She slipped on a pair of jeans and light sweater.

She walked out into the living room and into the kitchen. Romeo was putting two plates on the table. The smell of eggs, bacon and biscuits assaulted her senses, and her stomach rumbled loudly. She walked over to the counter.

"Do you want coffee?" she asked as she pulled over the sugar canister from the other side.

"Please. The cups are on the right, and the cream is in the fridge." She jumped at the brief contact as he brushed against her. He seemed not to notice as he turned to bring the silverware to the table. She poured two cups and put them on the table, then went back and got the sugar and cream and returned. They sat and ate in silence, and she was able to sneak little glances at him, although she was aware he was quite attentive to what she was doing.

She stood and took the plates to the sink. He walked up behind her and placed his arms around her waist and brought her back against him. He slowly bent his head to her ear and whispered, "It is good to know that you enjoy my touch. I can tell by the increase in your heart rate when I touch you. There will be more this evening, my dear, and you will never want to leave my bed. I am going to go get the car. Come out when you are ready. I am going to show you the beauty of the mountains. Then, I will take you to your estate." He slowly kissed her neck before pulling away and going to the door.

She looked down to see her hands were gripping the counter tightly. Was this real, or had she passed out when she got here and was still dreaming? She washed the dishes and placed them in the drainer before walking out onto the little porch to see a huge black Ford F250 high in the air next to her car. She should have known he would drive a lifted truck like that.

Romeo opened the door for her. Reaching out to give her his hand, he then helped her up into the seat. The truck roared to life as he started it up. He took her in the opposite direction she came from, and they rode for what seemed like forever on a little dirt road before pulling over and coming to a stop under a tree.

He suddenly hopped out of the truck. They were on the side of the road. What was he doing? Did he have to pee? Her door opened, and he reached up to grasp her hips and hoist her out of the truck. She slowly slid down the length of his body and looked up to see the mischievous grin on his face. *Men!*

He took her by the hand and led her into the trees in front of them. They walked through the woods until they came to a clearing with a huge beautiful lake, and a tall tree that shaded the ground. They proceeded to walk around the lake to the other side.

"When it is warmer, we will enjoy the lake, maybe with a picnic." He smiled down at her. Amanda saw herself there with him in the warm sunlight. She didn't even know this man, and she had already let him do more things to her than she should have.

They walked through the next set of trees and came to a huge cliff. The view was breathtaking. Beyond, she could see the snow-tipped mountains and a broad expanse of valley. Birds flew around them, and the sounds of animals could be heard from all around. She looked to him with a smile of wonder and saw his returning smile.

"I thought you might like it. I come here when I need to think," Romeo confessed.

"Oh, look at the happy little couple," same a sneer behind them. They turned to see a man with dark, long hair and emerald green eyes. He was very handsome, but the sneer on his face took away any appeal he may have had.

Romeo quickly shoved her behind him. She tried to peer over his shoulder to see the man.

"Enjoy her while you can, Romeo. Soon she will be mine and will never bare your children." The man gave a wicked grin in her direction.

She gripped Romeo's biceps and put herself flush against him.

"You will have to go through me first, Remus," Romeo said stiffly.

"Oh, that can be arranged." Remus gave her an even broader smile. "I will have her and your pack soon enough." Without another word, he disappeared back into the trees.

Romeo pulled out his phone and spoke in soft tones before shutting it and shoving it into his pocket. "Come on, let's get back to the cabin. It has now become apparent that your safety is in even more jeopardy than we thought." He grabbed her hand and started walking at a rather fast pace.

She tripped over her own feet to keep up with him. When they got to the truck, she placed her hands on the hood and panted to try and catch her breath. "Well, if he wasn't going to kill me, you almost did by exertion."

Suddenly, he was right in front of her with his face close to hers. "You would be wise to watch what you say. You do not know the man we are now dealing with. Rape would be the least of your worries with the torture he would perform on you." Romeo crushed his lips to hers and abruptly drew away.

Pulling her to the side of the truck, he hoisted her up to place her in the seat and walked quickly to his side and jumped up into the seat. The engine roared to life, and they headed back to the cabin.

"I need to go to my aunt's house," she protested. "There are things I need to do while I am here, and playing house with you isn't one of them."

"Is that so?" he asked, raising an eyebrow.

"Yes, it is. And, oh, just take me to her estate!" Amanda could hear herself becoming whiny.

"Fine, I will. But you need to become more accustomed to calling it *your* estate."

He was right. The estate now belonged to her. She was the owner of an estate. She shook her head as she tried to wrap her head around the idea of this money and family legacy stuff. She gave him a blank stare and nodded. Her life had changed so drastically in the last few days that it was hard to take it all in. All she could do was tell herself to breathe.

Chapter Four

The ride to the estate took about an hour. When they pulled up to the large iron fence, she gasped at the size of the gate alone. It was large with intricate designs engraved into it. There was a loud squeak as the massive doors opened wide for them to drive through. She looked up at the most beautiful and massive mansion she had ever seen.

When the attorney had told her it was more than just a home, she hadn't understood. Now, as she looked up at it, she instantly knew that what he had said was completely true. It was more than a house. It wasn't just some stone and pillars either. It was her family estate. A family that until two days ago she didn't even know she had. A family that brought with it a ton of different things she had never even thought possible or believed to be real. How could she? Who would have ever thought that werewolves were real? Then, she looked up to see Romeo staring down at her thoughtfully.

"What?"

He was looking at her strangely. She could see traces of worry on his face. Could he really be worried about her? He didn't even know her. Sure, he may have watched her from a distance, but he had never gotten to know her.

"You don't know me, Romeo." It came out like a sudden epiphany, like she was finally thinking straight.

"Sure I do. Your favorite color is blue. I can tell because you wear it all the time. You have a compassionate nature because of your profession and love for animals. You also are headstrong and stubborn but know what you want and stand up for what you believe in, and last, I know your lips are soft and sweet." He grinned.

She blushed and quickly turned from him, changing the subject. "I am just trying to take it all in. This is actually a lot, you know. I find out I have this mysterious family that I know nothing about. It is something that my family has kept from me my entire life. Now, I am looking at a castle that I am told belongs to me, and finally, I find out that my family is able to turn into dogs. I can't believe they kept this from me my whole life. What, did they not think that I would find out? "

"I think, my dear, they thought they would be here for you when the time came for this talk. It would have been this year, when you turned twenty-four. You are untouched and, because of that, you will now become a breeder when you do go to bed with me." He grinned at her, and she couldn't help the smile that crossed her face in return. No matter how much she wanted to hate him, she couldn't.

"Come on. Let's go look at this estate."

"Okay. You will love the library."

She stopped and looked over at him in wonder. "You've been here before?"

"Well, of course. Our families have been close since the beginning. My father knew that your aunt was in trouble and tried to get her to leave and go into hiding. She refused. She was very courageous and headstrong. You would have liked each other. You are a lot alike and have a lot in common."

"Oh really? Like what?"

He looked at her sternly. "She refused to get married and succumb to the ways of the werewolf. There were many times that she told my father that his day in time was over, and he needed to let her enjoy her life. I am afraid that did not stop the men from coming after her." He looked at her pointedly. "She was also very beautiful, as you are, and had an aura about her that gave off the impression that she was who she was and did not hide behind anything or anyone. She lived life to the fullest and enjoyed the outdoors. She was one-of-a-kind in every way and a very special woman. There was only one time that I did not agree with her choice. That was when there were attacks on the estate nightly from wolves trying to get to her to mate with her."

He looked sad for a moment, like he was lost in the memory. She knew that he was traveling back in time to the day he now spoke of. What had her aunt done that he didn't approve of? What could she have done that he would be so upset about?

"Oh goodness. What did she do?"

"I will not tell you." His face was disapproving as he looked at her angrily. "It is something that you will not do; *ever*!"

She was taken aback by the harshness of his voice. She knew instantly that it was not something that she would do. Although, many people didn't agree with her, Amanda thought of herself as a chicken. She didn't go out on a limb, and she didn't have much confidence in herself or her abilities either. There was only one thing that she knew she was good at and that was her career.

"Please, tell me what she did," Amanda said softly, trying to coax him.

He took a deep breath. "She went to see a doctor outside town. In some fancy hotel. The man was a werewolf that she found through some connections of hers and your grandfather's. No one knew until after it was done. She had surgery so that she could never have offspring."

She gasped; it was obvious that he hadn't approved of her aunt's decision.

She thought she understood immediately why he hadn't agreed. The passing of one's lineage was apparently very important to werewolves and his community. Her Aunt Mabel had taken away one of the only ways that the Traverse name could be passed down through the generations. If it weren't for Amanda, then it would have stopped with her.

Amanda realized what she was thinking. She had to have a child. It would be expected of her if she stayed there. She would have to keep the family legacy alive somehow, and the only way would be to have a child to pass it down to.

"For one, that is something I could never do. Second, you have to look at things from her point of view. She probably thought she had no choice."

He shook his head. "No. There were plenty of wolves who would have married her and mated with her. Plenty of men who would have treated her right and gave her a good life. Instead, she chose to cut all of them out before even giving them a shot."

She laid her hand on his shoulder and felt the warmth of his skin seep into her own. "I am sure she had her reasons."

"Yeah, sure. Come on, let's get out, and we can walk through the house. I don't see Stephan's car, so he must not be here. It is late in the evening, and everyone has left except the security at the gate."

Amanda looked over to see him smiling at her and wiggling his eyebrows. She didn't know what she was going to do. How could she not be attracted to him? How was she going to keep her hands to herself, much less keep him from doing things to her? But if she was honest, she didn't even know that she wanted him to keep his hands to himself.

For so long she had been alone, and here was a community who wanted her. Maybe she could be happy here? She had some big decisions to make and fast.

Romeo was no longer smiling at her playfully but staring at her intensely. Sparks of fire leaped from his eyes as his gaze traveled over her body yet again. "If you don't stop looking at me like that, then I cannot be accounted for my actions."

"Hmmm?" She gasped at how fast he moved. One minute he was across the room and the next he was pressing her against the wall. She felt the cool stone against her back as she looked up at him and panted for breath. She could feel him through her clothes and knew he was stiff. He ground his hips into hers as he looked down into her eyes.

"I could take you right here on the floor; I want you that bad, but you deserve so much more, especially for your first time." His mouth swooped to take hers in a kiss. This time he didn't go in easy. He gave her everything, and she thought she would burn alive with the heat that consumed her body in her pleasure. He devoured her mouth, nipping at her lips, and both of them groaned. His hands wrapped around to grab both of her cheeks, one in each hand, and raised her so that she was level with him. Without thinking or caring, she wrapped her legs around his waist as he ground into her against the wall.

"You are so beautiful," he said with a groan.

"Yeah, okay." She was amazed, and then everything stopped. He drew his head back and looked at her.

He caressed her hair. "You *are* beautiful."

She dropped her legs back to the floor, and he helped to steady her as she got feeling back into them to stand. "I am plain, not to mention all the pounds I shouldn't be carrying. Come on, why do you want me anyway? You could have any girl you wanted. I mean, look at you." Her eyes smoldered again as they traveled across his body.

His chuckle brought her head back up to meet his eyes again. "I am glad you approve of me, and I choose you. I have watched you since you were young. Our parents do not know this, but there was something that drew me to you even as a kid. When I turned fifteen, I found out about you. Your aunt told me about your father and your birth. She showed me pictures of you. There was something that pulled me to you. I had to find you. I had to know you. Then, our fathers made a pact. It was something that I would see through no matter what. I had to have you at my side. You have always been beautiful to me, and you still are. For you are amazing, just as your aunt was."

"My aunt knew about me?" She felt the blush creep into her cheeks again at his words.

"Yes. She loved you very much, and although she couldn't see you, for your safety, she watched you grow through pictures. She was an amazing woman and taught me many things."

"You were very close to her, weren't you?" She looked over at the sadness that swept his face.

"Yes. Like I said, she was an amazing woman."

"I wish I could have met her."

"You did speak to her at your parents' funeral."

"What?"

"Yes. I stood beside her as she took your hands into her own."

Amanda looked around. There wasn't much that she remembered about her parents' funeral. She had been so distraught and emotional. There had, however, been numerous people at the funeral she didn't recognize, and she realized that they had been part of the wolf community her father had come from. Her head snapped up, and she looked at him as she remembered. "I remember her. She had long, dark, straight hair and dark, blue eyes. I had thought she looked like my father, but I knew that he didn't have any family, so I had pushed it aside. She was his sister. I don't remember what she said."

He smiled at her. "She said that all things will be revealed to you soon. She said to know that you are loved and you will know your rightful place in due time. She said to be strong and hold on to your amazing parents' memories. As long as you remember them, they will forever be alive. She said she would see you again soon and everything in your life would make sense. She then kissed you on your cheek, and we left. I watched you, though. Call me a stalker, but I needed to make sure you were alright."

Amanda didn't know what to say as emotions swirled in his eyes. Everything was starting to make more sense. "Well, let's go see where we will be living then."

Amanda stepped into the foyer and couldn't believe the beauty. On the walls that stretched down the halls were large paintings. A man who looked ruggedly handsome sat on a chair in one of the portraits. On either side of him stood two young boys; one older than the other. Sitting on the floor was a woman, who smiled back at her husband. She was beautiful, and in her arms was a baby girl in pink, who looked to be around one. Sitting in the man's lap was another little girl in a pretty pink frilly dress who looked to be around four. She was looking up at her father, laughing. He looked down at her as well. It seemed the whole family registered their attention on the two of them with smiles.

"They looked so happy together." She whispered it, but she knew that he heard. She knew the painting was old just by looking at the style of clothing.

"Yes. It was painted in 1884, when your ancestor Edgar built the house. Some things have changed within these walls, such as electricity and plumbing, but the foundation and walls are one and the same. Your estate, my dear, is over 100 years old."

She turned her eyes toward him, and smiling, he kissed her briefly on the lips before turning and taking her hand in his own. Slowly, he began pulling her down the hall. There were paintings of families; all of her ancestors and relatives smiling back at her.

Ancestry.com, eat your heart out. Here was her family tree where she could see them all. They came to the last painting on the wall and she stopped. Staring at it, her hand reached up on its own to caress the face of the little boy in the painting. She knew instantly who it was.

"Your father was a great man, Amanda."

"I know. I just wish……"

"I know, little one. I know." He pulled her to the next space on the wall. It held a frame but no picture inside. "This is where our picture will go. I hope you want children."

"I never really thought about it." She fell into step with him. She was going along with everything like she was staying, but it wasn't exactly fair to him. She needed to figure out what she was going to do and fast.

"I want at least five." He turned to her with a sheepish grin.

"My gosh, that's a lot!" She looked at him, worriedly. She hadn't even wrapped her head around one yet.

"Yeah, but that just means more practice and the more times we get to try." His eyebrows wiggled over at her.

She couldn't help the laugh that exploded from her mouth. "You are insatiable."

"You have no idea, my dear." The smoldering look he gave her had her breath catching in her throat. Her body heated up all over again, and the blush crept back into her cheeks. "I love it that you still blush." His hands wrapped around her waist as he pulled her to him and kissed her deeply. She stood on her tiptoes as she kissed him back. "We need to stop before we take it much further. I will have you upstairs in our room before you know it, with you lying naked beneath me."

"Really? I mean, there is a room already designated for us?"

"Yes. Want to see it?"

She looked at his eyes and saw the passion. She knew he wanted her, and she wanted him just as badly. Would it be wise to be standing in a bedroom that was supposed to be theirs alone with him with the feelings she was starting to develop for him? She didn't think it would, but of its own accord, her head quickly nodded her approval. He smiled as he took her hand again and led her to the stairs.

Upstairs was a long hallway, showing off door after door, which she assumed to be bedrooms. They reached the end of the hall. There was another set of stairs going down the side which he explained led to the servants' quarters. He explained that her three times great-grandmother had died of cholera, and her husband had the stairs put in so that the servants could reach her more quickly when she needed them.

He opened the door and held it while she walked through. The room was huge and beautiful, as to be expected. There was a long dresser and a very large chest as well as a wooden hope chest at the foot of the bed. The floor was made of stone, and there was a huge fireplace in the corner. The massive television across from the bed looked way out of place in the practically antique room. But even with all the beauty to look at, it was the bed in the center that caught her attention.

It was massive and could have easily held five people or more. The large posts matched the dressers, and tied to the poles was a sheer white canopy. She felt like she was in a spell as she made her way to the bed. Sitting down, she looked over at him and smiled.

"This is amazing. It is so beautiful."

"It was brought over from France by your great-great-grandfather. He got rid of the furniture where his mother took her last breath. He had the whole place cleaned from top to bottom and had new furniture bought for the whole castle. Only the paintings and the dining room furniture and a couple chairs in the parlor are original. Oh, and the library. Everything is original in there as well. Of course, the mattress is new."

"Wow. This is like a cloud." She lay back on the mattress, not knowing the mistake she made. She was now positioned in the same way that he said he wanted to have her downstairs. The only problem was she wasn't naked. She opened her eyes to see his gaze traveling over her body again. Neither said a word as he made his way over to her. He sat beside her on the bed and his hand traveled down the front of her shirt. She laid perfectly still, afraid that if she moved he would stop. His gaze held hers as his hand slipped under her shirt to caress her stomach and then squeeze her side.

"We need to go now."

"Why?" She looked at him worriedly.

"Shit." He took her mouth with his own, kissing her deeply and, not caring anymore, she kissed him back with everything she had. Her arms wound around his neck to toy with the hair at the nape. He growled deep in his throat as his lips left hers. He kissed his way down the side of her neck, and she moaned as she pushed against him, wanting to be closer. She was partly in the middle of the bed, so she scooted over to make room for him. Her body turned toward his as he laid down beside her. He quickly removed her shirt and stared down at her breasts. She instantly felt self-conscious and tried to cover herself.

Looking back up at her, he pulled her hands from her body. "Never try to hide yourself from me. You are exquisite."

She couldn't even say a word at the intensity in his gaze. She let him pull her hands from her breasts before his lips descended onto her already hardened nipple through the fabric of her bra.

Suddenly everything in the home went dark. She jerked with fear and jumped up. He stood and walked around, trying to flick the lights on and off. Nothing happened.

"What is going on?" She sat up on the bed, quickly.

"Electricity is out." He walked over to pick up some matches and lit a hanging lantern by the door. Walking over to the fireplace that was stacked with firewood, he began to start a fire. Within minutes, he had large flames licking at the stone as a fire came dancing to life.

"Well, this is just great." Amanda threw her hands into the air. Rising from the bed, she quickly walked up to Romeo, not paying attention to her state of undress. She was frustrated as her arms raised into the air again. "What do we do now?"

"Easy. This." He pulled her to him as his mouth captured hers. He swallowed the small gasp as his tongue slipped between her lips. He licked at the depths of her mouth and gathered her even closer at her moan. His hands trailed down to grip her ass and bring her flush up against him. She wrapped her arms around his neck and hung on.

He lifted her as she jumped up and wrapped her legs around his waist as he pushed her up against the wall. "My god, what I want to do to you. I want to be deep inside you now. You feel so good."

"Then, hurry." She felt wobbly as she dropped her feet back to the floor and stood unsteady for a minute. She smiled at him as he looked down at her again. She giggled when he sucked in a deep breath.

The lace-covered bra was completely see-through and dark blue. It contrasted perfectly against her smooth white skin and matched her eyes. Her hands glided up his chest and removed his shirt. He seemed for a moment to be almost as nervous and shaky as she was.

Before she could give it another thought, her pants were gone, as well as her bra and panties. Romeo leaned above her, trailing kisses down her neck. A burning sensation swept across her body wherever his lips touched her skin. Leaning her head against the wall, she moaned deeply as he took a nipple in his mouth. He nibbled it with his teeth before sucking it into his mouth and finishing it with a long lick of his tongue. Taking his time, his lips and mouth traveled to the other breast, giving it the same attention.

He directed her to the bed and slowly removed his own clothes before joining her on the soft mattress. Leaning over her, he pushed her thighs wide apart and settled his hips against them. His shaft jutted at her entrance, and she felt him push the tip inside her. She held her breath. He pushed in farther and then stopped. She looked up and understood that he was at her maidenhead. She didn't say a word. All she could do was nod, giving him the permission he needed to take her.

He pushed forward. There was a searing pain inside of her. She whimpered slightly at the burning and agonizing pain she felt in the walls of her most private place. A tear slid from her eye, and he was right there to catch it quickly. He kissed her deeply, and she felt his hand at her clit, encircling it gently. The pain began to ebb away and was soon replaced with something else. The slow burn of ecstasy crept back again, and before she knew it, she was moving and moaning, wanting more of him.

He eased inside her until he was completely filling her to the hilt. She had never felt so full and complete. It was amazing, and she wanted more. She couldn't wait any longer as she wiggled against him.

Looking up at him, she saw his strained expression and knew he was holding back. She leaned up and licked against his bottom lip. "More."

All he could do was grunt as he gave her what she wanted. Easing out, he slammed back into her.

"Yes!"

He let go and slammed into her over and over. Something broke inside him, and he couldn't stop the onslaught of emotions as he took her with no mercy or restraint. Over and over, he slammed into her tight depths until she clenched around him.

Letting himself loose, he buried himself deep and groaned as he shuddered with the last of his release. It was like lightning and so intense she didn't know if she could make it through the orgasm. Looking at Romeo, she saw his wide eyes and knew instantly that he felt the same way. He didn't let her go, even after they were both spent. They were side by side now.

They laid there for a while before he left her lying on the bed. He came back a couple of minutes later with a rag in his hand. She instantly felt embarrassed as he pushed her legs apart. She tried closing them but he gave her a stern look.

"I will see and touch and feel every part of your body. From this day forward, you are not to hide from me ever. Do you understand?"

"I understand, but I am fully capable of cleaning myself."

"I want to." The breath she was holding came out in a hiss as he slid the cool cloth against her raging flesh. She felt sore, like she was on fire. The coolness of the cloth soothed her skin and felt amazing. He left to rinse the blood from the rag and wet it again before returning back to her side. He repeated it two more times until he thought it was good enough. Washing the rag out for the last time, he hung it on the edge of the sink and made his way back to the bed. He sank down beside her and threw a cover over the both of them. They were soon fast asleep with him holding her in his arms the whole time.

Chapter Five

Romeo awoke and looked down at the sleeping woman. She was beautiful, and he was ecstatic that she had chosen him, but he knew that it was time to wake her. They needed to get home so that she could meet his father. He had woken earlier and quickly called Mr. Montgomery, the attorney, to let him know that he had brought her to look over the house and he had a really good notion that she would be staying in their little town. The attorney told him how happy he was with her decision and that he would start getting all the paperwork together for her to sign off on it.

Amanda looked up at the man above her and smiled. He was lost in thought, and didn't even know that she was awake. He must have felt her staring at him because he looked down at her.

"I told Mr. Montgomery that you have decided to stay. He is drawing up the papers as we speak."

"What? Why did you do that?" She sat up quickly and raised the sheet to cover her nakedness from his view.

His forehead instantly drew into a frown. "I told you not to hide yourself from me."

"And I told you I was my own person. I will make my own decisions. I don't need some man that I don't even know choosing what I'm going to do with my life. What about my career? I went to school for a very long time to become a successful veterinarian. Who are you to tell me I can't chase my dreams?"

"I never said you couldn't chase your dreams, damn it. I just told him that you would be chasing them with me from now on."

"And how do you know that's what I want?"

"Because of what we just did, maybe. Because you know as well as I do that we were meant to be husband and wife. You know we were meant to spend the rest of our lives together and nothing can change that. Not now or ever."

"You are such an infuriating man or wolf, or whatever you are. You aggravate my patience to no end. No matter what you might think or either of our fathers think, I am my own woman, and there is no way in hell I am going to let any of you tell me how I should live my life or who in the hell I should marry. Got it? Now, if you will excuse me, I would like to look around some more before we head back."

"Fine, but there is just one more thing." His face was close to hers, and both of them threw sparks of anger at the other. What he had thought would be a lovely morning of more lovemaking had slowly turned into a battle between two vipers. There was no way in hell she would give in now, no matter what. Oh, he knew he could coerce her into making love again, but he didn't want that. He wanted her to come to him of her own free will. He wanted to hear the words come from her lips that she wanted him. That was definitely not something that would be happening this morning.

Amanda sat staring at the aggravating man. Who gave him the right to boss her around? She wasn't a child, and she wasn't his wife. This was the twenty-first century, not the 1800s, where women walked on eggshells to keep men happy. She would be damned if she'd bow down to anyone, including him. She would rather punch him square in the nose than give into him. Her face scrunched even more as she thought of giving in. No way. No how. Suddenly, the sheet was jerked away from her skin. The cold air left a path of goose bumps across her flesh where it hit her. She shivered with the unexpected coldness, and her eyes widened in shock.

"What do you think you are doing?"

"I am looking my fill at the woman who will be in my bed every night from now on."

"Oh, you don't listen, do you? Let me go."

"No, damn it. You will listen, and you will listen well. You are going to be my wife, no matter what. You were meant to be my wife. You will be my wife!"

She screeched as his arms wrapped around her and brought her flush against him. His lips crushed hers to his. This wasn't a gentle and sweet kiss like the ones from before. This was pure anger melted into some intense desire. His lips probed hers until she gave in on a gasp and let his tongue enter to explore the recesses of her mouth. She moaned and started to lean in before he ripped his lips from hers.

Breathing deep, he looked at her angrily. "You want this as much as I do, but you are too damn stubborn to admit it. I just proved it. I know how you and your body responded to mine. Remember how it felt to be in my arms the next time you want to act like we don't belong together." He moved from the bed, and she watched silently as he yanked his clothes on in a hurry with impatient and angry gestures. As he stomped to the door, he turned around to look at her once more before turning and walking from the room.

Amanda sat there for a few minutes and thought about what he had said. He was right. She did want to stay. At least she thought she might. The only problem was she didn't like the choice being taken from her. She didn't like being told what she was going to do. She was her own person and had been living on her own for many years. The last seven years of her life had been lonely, but they had been her own. She didn't have to answer to anyone. She did what she wanted and went wherever she pleased. Now all of a sudden she was expected to answer for every move she made. That wasn't something that sat well with her. It made her angry, and she knew it would continue to make her angry in the future.

She rose from the bed gingerly. She was sore everywhere as she made her way over to her clothes. She looked around for her panties and bra. Picking up the white cloth that used to be her underwear, she sighed and pulled on her pants. She would have to go commando. She knew that night she would be hurting, for she was already sore, and the jeans definitely weren't going to feel good.

She made her way through the large house quietly and slowly. The designs in the wood furnishings and all throughout the house amazed her.

Upon reaching the outside, she saw that Romeo was standing against the truck. He gave her a blank stare. There was no emotion on his face.

They rode in silence until they came to the small cabin that belonged to Romeo. He helped her from the truck and kept his arm around her waist as they made their way to the door. Although they'd had an argument, he still kept her at his side, and she knew that he was a man any woman would be proud to call hers.

He opened the door to the cabin, and there were people everywhere. Joseph, Audri and Aurora, and three other men. The men parted to show an older man.

"Amanda, this is my father, Jeremiah," Romeo explained.

She looked at the gentlemen and could see his likeness to Romeo. He had the same darkness as Audri but had light blue eyes. He looked at her with a kind smile as he took both of her hands into his own. "Ah, you have the beauty of your mother but your father's eyes. It is good to finally meet you, my long lost goddaughter." He spoke with a deep voice. This man couldn't be older than his fifties and was strong and built like his sons.

"Thank you. It is good to finally meet someone from my parents' lives. They were very secretive, and I was never able to find any other family of my own," she said quietly.

He looked at her with sadness. "Yes, my child. I am sorry to tell you that your aunt was the last of a lineage. You see, your uncle and grandparents were killed many years ago. My father found your father and aunt and hid them from the other communities. My parents raised them as their own, and I knew them as my younger siblings. It wasn't until they were older that our pack helped them take their family home back over and the Traverse legacy into their hands. Your mother's family disowned her when they found that she had married a werewolf. I am sure you don't know this, child, but you are a rare individual. Part werewolf and part witch." He gazed at her solemnly.

"What? First I learn that my father was a werewolf, now I learn that he was a witch, too, and that I may still have family out there?" she asked with both shock and frustration.

"No, my child; your father was a werewolf and your mother was a very powerful witch." He smiled, took her hand and led her to the couch. "First, let me introduce my family to you. You have met Romeo, Joseph, and the girls," he announced with a wave of his hand.

Suddenly, a man who was casually leaning against the wall walked to her. "I am Sebastian," He had dark hair that hung to his shoulders and dark blue eyes. He bowed before her. "I am at your disposal, ma'am." He went to go back to the other side of the room to prop himself into his earlier position.

Another man stepped forward. "I am Elijah. I am glad to meet you. Welcome to the family." He looked more like Romeo, with light brown hair that was shorter than all the others and a smile across his face.

"I am Bryce." The next one had long brown hair and a likeness to Joseph. He wore a grin as he said; "I am willing to help you, my dear, with anything you may need." He gently took her hand and grazed the knuckles with his lips. She heard a deep growl from behind her and turned to see a murderous look focused in his direction from Romeo.

"Bryce, stop antagonizing your brother," Jeremiah ordered, with a push to Bryce's shoulder.

Bryce laughed as he looked at Romeo. "He needs to lighten up. He's always so moody and brooding."

"You're telling me," she whispered and realized everyone heard when they all turned to her. Bryce and Joseph burst out laughing, and Jeremiah chuckled.

"She's already got you pegged, big brother," Joseph said with a slap to his back.

Romeo turned his smoldering look her way and stated in a matter of fact way; "No, not yet, but she will soon enough." He raised his eyebrows, and she caught the hidden meaning behind it. She felt herself flush, and she hoped nobody else around her understood. Though, she was sure they did.

They may have had sex in the mansion, but she knew there was still a lot she didn't know about sex. She knew that he wanted to show her a lot more. Not only could she feel it but he had told her so many times before. His eyes held a different meaning when she met them with her own. She quickly averted her gaze before her body went up in flames right there in front of his family.

Jeremiah cleared his throat. "I know this is very hard to believe, my dear, so I brought some things to show you."

Bryce brought him a large wooden box that had been sitting against the wall. He slowly opened it and brought out a stack of pictures and handed them to her. She saw pictures of two boys with a young girl, then three teenagers and then two adult men and an adult woman. The last pictures were of a man and woman; her parents. She felt the tears rolling down her cheeks.

She looked up and realized she was suddenly alone with Jeremiah. "I miss them so much. I remember my mother smelling of lilacs. Every time I smell them, I think of her. My father was quiet, but he read to me as a kid, and I still have his car. I couldn't get rid of it. God, I miss them."

"I know, my dear. Your parents were taken away too soon," he said with tears in his eyes.

Finally, everything fell into place, and she realized that the truth was right there in front of her.

"I have many stories of your mother and father I can share with you. Your mother and father met when they were sixteen and fell madly in love with each other. Although the wolf community welcomed your mother as your father's mate, her family did not. It was very hard on her to leave her family behind. When other communities found out that your father was alive, they left the country and fled. They lived in Europe for many years until you were conceived. When your mother found out that she was pregnant, they changed their identities and came back to settle close to their roots. I am afraid the other communities must have found out who your father was. Your mother's people have never known about you. I know you do have an uncle on your mother's side, but after your parents' death, I stopped looking. Your mother had more powers than any ordinary witch did, my dear, and if you carry the powers, which I am sure you do, you will start growing into them soon."

"So, you have been watching me my whole life? Why not tell me who you were? Why not explain this to me a long time ago?" she asked, perplexed.

"Because even though I believe some knew of you, many of the other communities did not know of your existence. If I got close to you, knowing who your father was to me, then they would have looked farther into it, and you would have been placed in great danger. I missed your father a great deal after they fled. He was not only my friend, but my brother as well. Your aunt, however, mourned the most. You see, her other family was killed and taken from her when she was but a child, and now her only living relative had been taken as well. I believe that is why she never married. She couldn't bear to lose anyone else. That, and she was in love with Stephan."

"You mean the butler? She was in love with him?"

"There were things said, and to this day he refuses to leave the place, stating that he will serve the next family in the home. He told me at her funeral that he couldn't bear to leave the one place where he was truly happy. He said your aunt brought light into his old dark world, and he will be forever grateful. Many people did not agree with her having him on the estate."

"Why? Is he a bad werewolf or something?"

"No, my dear. He is a human. Many wolves believed him to be a vampire, but it was never proven. Who knows?"

"A what? You have got to be kidding me, right?" How many more bombs were going to be dropped on her safe world?

"No, dear. They are real; just as many creatures of the night are that you don't even know about."

"There really are people out there that suck blood and people who turn into wolves." She was shaking her head in wonder.

"Not just wolves, my dear." He smiled at her cautious look. "Were-people are out there in numerous places. There are werewolves, weresnakes, werepanthers and even weretoads, among other animals. Our species is just more obvious because of stupid individuals who wanted fame and glory." He shook his head in disgust. That was apparently a topic for another time.

"So, keeping me here, having me marry Romeo, is putting your family in danger as well then?" she asked.

"Yes. But we are aware of what we are doing and prepared to do what we must. You were always meant to marry my son and be the alpha queen. You were to be a part of our family, no matter how it happened. We stand by our family, my dear. There are over 200 wolves in our community who stand behind you as their queen and will fight to the death if need be for you." His voice was stern.

"This is just so much," she said as she stood.

"I know, my dear, and I am sorry, but we are running out of time now. The full moon is upon us." He handed her the pictures he had shown her. "These are for you. You will cherish them more than I. I am an old man who misses his brother and sister, but you have lost your parents. But know this; you have just gained not only a husband and family, but an entire community as well." He stood up and hugged her before walking to the door.

Chapter Six

Amanda heard the door shut behind Jeremiah and looked through the pictures again. She stood there with tears rolling down her cheeks and suddenly felt hands slide up her arms. She knew instantly it was Romeo. She turned around and went into his arms. She cried like the day she lost her parents as he held her and rubbed his hands down her back.

"Shih, it will be okay. I am here, as well as my family, and we will not let anything happen to you," he comforted quietly as he kissed her temple.

Her sniffles finally quieted. "What if you were not told to marry me? Would you still want me? I mean, it seems that you have been pushed into this as well." It seemed like a fair question.

He chuckled. "My dear, I have been watching you since I was a boy. There was nobody else for me. I have known many women, but I will only have one wife, and I have always known that woman would be you."

She looked at him with wide eyes, wrapping her hands around his neck and stood on her tiptoes to bring his mouth down to her own. It was tentative at first; just a brief little touch. Suddenly, he hauled her against him and kissed her with such force and passion that she could barely breath. He lifted her and carried her to the bedroom. She knew deep down that this was going to happen. If she was honest with herself, she could say she knew from the first time she spoke to him.

He set her down beside the bed and pulled back. His smoldering gaze met hers as he lifted her shirt from over her head. Her hands instinctively went to the bottom hem of his shirt, and he helped her to pull it off. She ran her hands across his chest, stopping to circle little scars here and there. He pulled her into his arms and reached his right hand around to unclasp her bra with a flick of his wrist. As her bra fell, she could feel the warm heat of his body pressed against her own as her nipples grazed his chest. He gently closed one hand around her right breast and bent his head to take it into his mouth. Gently, he grazed it with his teeth.

She leaned her head back with a groan. His other hand curled around her ass and squeezed first one cheek and then the other. He stood back up to take her mouth again as his hands made quick work with her zipper and buttons. She suddenly stood there in nothing but a pair of white panties.

"God, you are beautiful," he whispered. His hands went to the zipper on his own jeans. She sat on the bed and scooted back, coming up to her knees. Suddenly, she didn't feel embarrassed by her body. She didn't feel like she needed to hide herself from his gaze.

He slowly unbuttoned the jeans and slid the zipper down. Hooking his fingers in the sides of his boxers, he slowly lowered both to the floor. He looked to her with a wicked grin when she took in the full expanse of his body. He was all muscle without an ounce of fat. His body was lightly tan, even though it was fall. She slowly slid her eyes down his chest and rippled stomach to rest at the juncture of his thighs. His cock stood erect and ready. Her heart skipped a beat as he came slowly toward her, crawling like a predator across the bed. He grabbed her ankles and pulled her to him.

"First, these have got to go," he growled as he grabbed the sides of her panties, and with a small pull, ripped them completely off and flung them behind him.

"Hey, I liked those," she joked.

"Yeah? I'll buy you some new ones. I like to see this even better." He slowly pushed her thighs apart and ran his finger through her slit. She moaned softly. "I told you I would have you today," he warned before his lips grazed her stomach.

He slowly licked his way down her bikini line and back and opened her lips. He flicked her clit with his tongue, and she came off the bed. Placing his arm over her stomach, he smiled wickedly at her as he held her in place so that she couldn't move away from him.

"Ah, ah, ah, no moving," he scolded seductively. She leaned her head back against the pillows and grabbed the sheet on both sides of her as she felt him take long licks up and down her slit.

"Please," she begged, softly.

He pushed one finger inside her then another. As he caught a slow rhythm, he took her clit into his mouth and gently sucked. Next, he replaced his finger with his tongue and put pressure on her clit with his thumb.

"Oh, oh my god." She moaned and writhed on the bed, tossing her head from side to side. He was killing her. "If I don't come soon I'm gonna die. Please!" she pleaded.

He looked up into her face as he placed his fingers back inside her, stroking gently. He leaned down and started pumping his fingers harder and faster.

She closed her eyes and felt his mouth return to her clit. He gently sucked and then harder until she exploded. He took three long licks up her slit before he raised himself above her. He looked down into her face as he caressed her body. He made circles on her nipples with the palm of his hand and bent down to kiss her. She tasted herself on his lips and pulled him down closer. She opened her legs and wrapped them around his waist. Two could play this game.

Amanda broke away from the kiss to gently kiss, suck and nip at the side of his throat. She then lifted her hips, seeking. She heard his loud moan when she wrapped her fingers around his hard shaft. Slowly, she guided it to her wet center.

"Would you please take me now?" she whispered into his ear.

With a low growl, he shoved her to the bed. His hands were everywhere, and she felt him sink inside her. He eased into her tortuously slow. He kept easing inside her until she was full. Looking down, he framed her face with his hands. She lifted her hips off the bed, trying to get him deeper.

He moaned loudly. "Stay still or I will lose control." His teeth were clenched as he spoke.

"Hmmm," he said with a wicked grin. He looked down at her. He began to pull out, and she started to stop him but then suddenly he pushed back inside her in one fluid movement. She moaned loudly and closed her eyes for a second. When she opened them back up he was staring at her as he slowly moved in and out.

"Lose control, Romeo. Take me like you really want to."

Suddenly, he had her leg gripped behind the knee, and he bent her leg up to her chest with his amazing strength. He started pumping his hips faster and harder. She thought she was going to die.

"Oh, god, yes. Don't stop," she yelled.

"Oh, I won't, baby. I promise you that. My god, yes!" he panted above her. Sweat was trickling down his temples. Suddenly, he pulled out and flipped her over onto her stomach. Wrapping his arm around her waist, he raised her up on all fours. He slid inside her again and gripped her hips to bring her back against him. She arched her back, giving him more access. He gripped her hips almost painfully and brought her sharp against him. Holding her in place, he pounded into her.

There was force behind every push, and she leaned down onto her elbows to help brace herself.

She was gripping the sheets and arched her back as she exploded into the biggest orgasm she had ever had. Romeo followed shortly after, with a shout of his own. He slowly pumped into her a few more times as he grazed the back of her legs with his nails, running them up and down a few times. He arose from the bed as she slumped down where she was to roll over to her side. She looked up at him in wonder as he grinned at her.

"Come on. Let's go take a shower. You need to sleep," he offered gently. She realized with everything that had happened it had gotten late. It was a full moon, and she knew he would be Changing tonight.

He turned on the shower and turned to help her in beside him. He slowly ran his hands up and down her body and washed every part of her. When he was done, she did the same for him. After she was finished, she turned to face him with a wicked little smile. She dropped to her knees in front of him and took him in her hands. He braced his hands on the shower walls and looked at her with wide eyes. She slowly slid her tongue across the top of the smooth head and smiled with pleasure at his small gasp. She then slid her tongue under the head and started from the base of his shaft and licked all the way to the top.

One of his hands gripped her by the hair as the other planted itself on the wall. He brought her lips to the tip, and she smiled up at him as she took it into her mouth. She took him as deep as she could until he hit the very back of her throat. She slowly swallowed a couple times for him to feel the sensation against the head. He groaned loudly, and she slowly slid him almost completely out of her mouth. Then, she repeated the process.

"Oh god. If you don't finish I'm gonna have you against this wall," he told her breathlessly.

She smiled up at him innocently.

Suddenly he gripped her by the elbows and hauled her up against the wall of the shower. Before she knew what was happening, he was inside her again. He took her nipple into his mouth and sucked urgently as he rammed into her. She wrapped her legs around him. This time was not gentle or sweet. It was purely primal. He rammed into her hard, and she took every inch while begging for more and more. They both exploded together while kissing and screaming into each other's mouths.

Her legs were jelly as she tried to stand. He steadied her and quickly washed them both again. She hadn't realized that the water was starting to turn cold. He helped her from the shower and quickly dried them both off. He picked her up and carried her to the bed, gently pulling back the covers. He laid her down and then followed her under the covers.

"Rest. Tonight is going to be stressful for you. It will be the first time you see the form of your people. You need to be ready for that," he whispered and gathered her close.

"Will I be ready? What's going to happen now?" she asked quietly.

"You will be my wife and bear my children."

She sighed before they both fell asleep.

Chapter Seven

Amanda woke the next morning and made her way downstairs, surprised to see that Romeo wasn't there. She grabbed a muffin and made a quick cup of coffee. After her rushed breakfast, she made her way to her car and began the trek to her new home. She was glad she had kept the directions the attorney had given her a couple of days ago. She came to the gate, and the man knew instantly who she was.

"Good morning, ma'am."

"Good morning. I wanted to come back and take a look around again."

"Yes, ma'am. You let us know if you need help with anything, okay?"

She smiled at him. "Thank you. I will."

When Amanda got to the house, she made her way up the long staircase. She had decided she would start with the upstairs and work her way down. She was amazed yet again at how beautiful the place was. She felt like a little kid in a candy store and was more excited with each step she took.

One room had been done in all blue, another in pink. Still others in yellow and green. That was the extent of the colored rooms, however, for as she continued on, the rooms were decorated in flowers or beach scenes. They were all unique and beautifully designed. All fifteen bedrooms were equipped with a long dresser, large bed, tall dresser and hope chest in different kinds of woods. None, however, were made with the same deep mahogany wood that her furniture was.

She came to a door that was closed and almost turned away. Realizing that this was her house now, she decided that she could go anywhere she wanted to. The large room was a storage area of some sort. There was a small desk in one corner. The rest of the room was laden with shelves. Each of the shelves were stacked high with books. As she got closer, she realized that the books were all done in the same dark brown leather.

With her curiosity getting the better of her, she pulled the first one down and opened it. She gasped at what she saw.

May 2, 1884

The house is almost built, and I am happy to say that I am quite pleased with it. My dear Adrian will love it when I ask for her hand. She is at a young age but will make a fine wife. The furnishings belonging to my new home will be arriving within the month, and I will be most happy to finally settle. The boarding house in town is nice, but not for me. I like to be able to let my wolf run free. I have noticed other were-species in these parts, but I do not know if they are hostile or not. Adrian's father has told me that there are but a few werewolves left in these mountains. I will be glad to finally see her as my wife and spread our pack out across the expanse of the mountainside.

The days are long now, and the sun seems to stay up in the sky longer than before. The air is also much warmer, and it is the perfect time to start the interior of my home, including the painting. With the warmth in the air, the paint will dry much quicker. I remember the dampness from back home and how dreary it looked. I am glad that there is sunshine that floats into the valley of the mountains. I have traveled to Widow's Peak many times over the months I have been here. It is a beautiful place and the highest point on my land. Of the 312 acres, the mountains are contained on at least two-thirds of the total. This will give me and my pack the freedom to run and hunt in wolf form. I am looking forward to spending my years here with my family and can't wait until everything is done and we are moved safely in.

Until my next thoughts, I bid adieu.

Amanda was amazed at what she read. Could this really be her ancestor? The book had apparently been read many times before, since the pages were becoming worn. She decided to sit at the desk and carried the book back with her, flipping to the next page. She was amazed at how intelligent Edgar was. He must have had much schooling.

May 15, 1884

The house is finally painted and ready to be moved into. Adrian, however, has decided that I may not be the husband she wants. I have caught her with the saloon owner, Curly, multiple times and have decided she is not the woman that I thought she was. She, however, seems to think I am an idiot. She tells me that her feelings are for me alone and that her actions were foolish and done on a whim. I am no fool and have started to look elsewhere.

The town has become increasingly dangerous. I have noticed that were-people are not the only supernaturals in the valley. Witches and vampires are coming out of the woodwork and I am not too happy with the way they treat the were-people and humans in the town. I have called upon the help of my brothers. Antonius, Benjamin and Zachariah have told me they will help. They will be arriving within the next two months to help solve the problems in the town. The people of the small town in Slatesville have looked to me and made me the mayor of the town to keep it safe from the riff-raff who have started to show themselves in the streets. I only hope that I can make them proud and keep it safe for them to stay and live peacefully.

Until my next thoughts, I bid adieu.

Amanda sat back in the chair. She was amazed at the content in the letters. She needed to read all of them. As she looked around, she realized that there were thousands upon thousands of books. She didn't know if she could read them all before she died. She looked down at the book and knew that everything she needed to know about herself and her family was held in between those pages. She was curious to know when he stopped writing in his journals. Making her way to the last set of shelves; she knelt down to pull the last book from the slot. It was made of a different kind of leather and opening it, she gasped.

The writing was different, and she realized that it was no longer Edgar writing in the books.

June 1, 2013

I am writing because it will soon be time for me to pass the torch. My dear niece is not aware of the ways of our family, and I believe it is time that I brought her here and told her of the things she does not know. She has just graduated from college. She thinks that she did not have any family there to cheer her on, and it kills me that she was not aware that I sat there in the audience with Romeo at my side. He will make her a good husband and teach her the ways of our people. My heart filled with pride and joy as she walked across the stage. I knew my brother also watched her with pride from the afterlife. She will bring much to our family name, and our ancestors will be proud to call her family.

Stephan has begun to worry over me more. I cannot believe he has stayed with me all this time. He loves me so, as I do him. I could not see my life without him at my side. He is my life. He believes he is not good enough because he is but a mere human. I say he is wrong. He refuses to marry me and says that it will only cause me more harm than good. He still comes to my bed and holds me through the night as he did when we were kids. My brother would have skinned him alive if he had known the liberties I let Stephan get away with. I loved him then, and I love him now. He will forever be the only man for me, in my heart and in my bed.

I know that when I am gone, he will look over Amanda. Although my brother changed her name to Walker, I can only hope that she knows she is truly a Traverse by blood and heart. I fear for her safety from her mother's people. They are not good people, and the magical convent is looking for Radiants. If my suspicions are correct, then her mother passed the gene down to her, and she holds more power in her pinky than most witches do in their whole body. I fear for her sanity. There is a lot for her to take in, and I only pray that she will be able to see the joy in being who she is. She is strong, and I know she will see it through. She is the next in our legacy. She holds the key to our survival, not only as a family, but as a legacy and pack as well.

Until my next thoughts, I bid adieu.

Tears streamed from her eyes as she read on the next few pages. Her aunt was a very special woman who had cared a lot for her older brother. It had apparently torn her apart when he left to be with Amanda's mother. She also read about the intense love that she had shared with Stephan, her butler. He had doted on her, and she was amazed at the odds the two of them had fought just to be together. They had shared a love that was pure and true. Amanda wondered what it was like to have someone love you so much that they continued to be a servant until their dying day. She also knew that Stephan was probably in much pain since her aunt's death. He had continued to come to the house, however, and she knew that she must tell him to take a break to grieve.

Amanda rose and quietly made her way to the front of the home. She was so lost in thought that the front door opening behind her startled her.

"Who are you, and what in the hell are you doing here?"

She turned at the hard and accusing voice and saw the shock as it registered on the stranger's face. His posture instantly straightened as he looked at her. "I am so sorry. You must be Amanda."

"Yes, I am. How did you know?"

"You look like your father and aunt, ma'am. You have your mother's eyes but the Traverse features, just like my Mabel did." His eyes instantly widened at the slip up he just made. "I mean Ms. Mabel. Uh, your aunt." He tried to cover it back up, but he looked uneasy as he knew the cat was out of the bag, so to speak.

"It is okay, Stephan. I know of your relationship with my aunt."

"You do?" He looked at her worriedly. "I am a great butler, ma'am. I would love to serve you. Please don't make me leave. This house is all I have left of her. That, and my memories. I need to be close to her for my own sanity. She was taken too early."

Tears seeped from the old man's eyes, and Amanda got a good look at him for the first time. He was wearing a suit, but she knew that by the look of it he had dried it instead of pressing it. His hair was a little rumpled but not necessarily messy. However, his eyes were the worst. They were rimmed in red from tears that he had shed over the past few days, and there were dark circles from the lack of sleep. Her heart twisted at his pain. She instantly felt the need to help him. Walking up to him, she took both of his hands into her own.

"You are free to stay here as long as you like, Stephan. I will never ask you to leave. This home is as much yours as it is mine. You were a big part of my aunt's life, and I know you are grieving. Why don't you stay here for the time being? You can just relax and mourn your loss. I know you used to go to her room at night. Would you like to stay in her room?"

His eyes clouded as tears ran from the corners. "I would love that, ma'am. I come here every day to lie in the bed. It still smells of her in the room, and I feel close to her as long as I can smell her. I know it is weird and sounds strange. I just don't think I am ready to let her go quite yet."

"I am sure. How about you take your time, and when you are ready, I would love it if you could tell me about her. You knew her better than anyone, and I want to know about her. She was apparently a remarkable woman from what Romeo tells me."

"Yes, she was. Romeo was good with her. They had a bond as well, although it was more like mother and son. He lost his mother at a young age, and I think that

Mabel kind of filled that gap a little for him. He, in turn, gave her the family she lacked and needed. She was able to pass down your family history to him. Knowing that you two would one day be married she was happy to share with him, knowing it would one day go on to you. Thank you, ma'am."

"There is but one condition I have with the whole thing."

"And what is that, ma'am?"

"You stop calling me ma'am and call me Amanda." Her face split into a grin, and he smiled back at her.

"Yes, of course, ma…. Amanda."

"Okay then. I am going to go now. I am expected to be at Romeo's tonight, I presume. I don't know what is going on with these werewolves, but I don't really want to be alone."

'Yes…. Amanda. You have a good day, and I will see you soon."

"Yes, you have a good one."

She made her way back out to her car and was surprised to see that Romeo was there waiting on her. It seemed that no matter where she went, the man was always one step ahead of her. She didn't know if he had followed her, or if he had known where she was going. She was a little annoyed as she realized she would be watched no matter where she went. Would she have no privacy at all? Would she have to live a life where there was someone behind her at all times, or would the harassment ease as soon as she and Romeo mated?

"I thought you would be here. Although I know you like your freedom, I would ask that you not go out alone for the time being. This may be a fortress of sorts, but it cannot guarantee your safety, as me or one of my brothers could. I am sorry. I wish you could go alone and have your privacy; it is just not safe until we mate." She read the sadness in his eyes and knew that he really did want her to be happy, and he didn't like to have to follow her. They were both in a situation they didn't like, and all they could do was make the best of it.

"Okay then. Let's go back to your place for the time being." She held three of the books from the small storage room in her hand.

"What's that you got there?" He nodded at the books.

"Journals that belonged to my ancestor, Edgar, who built the house. I figure the best way to find out who I truly am is to read about my family. It seems that everyone in my family wrote journals, including my aunt."

"Wow. That's great, my dear. Now you can learn even more. We can head to my place, and you can start reading while I start making us something to eat. How's that sound?" He smiled at her. Apparently, he was relieved that she didn't get angry he followed her

"That sounds good." He helped her up into the truck before making his way around to his side and jumping into the seat. Starting the truck, he pulled away from the massive home. As they made their way to the gate, she looked back at the huge building. This was her home, her family and her legacy.

Chapter Eight

That night they lay in each other's arms again. They only had a few hours before the moon would be high in the sky and the ceremony could begin.

Suddenly, the door to the bedroom burst open and in walked three men she hadn't seen before. Behind them was the man who had been in the woods, Remus.

"Well, we meet again, my dear. Now, you will come with me," he announced with an evil grin. She shrank back against Romeo.

Suddenly, another man walked in, gripping a fighting Audri. "Let go of me, you son of a bitch!" she screamed.

"What do you want here, Remus?" Romeo said as he stood and pulled on his pants.

"Why, everything, Romeo. You took from me what was mine." He sounded so evil.

All three men grabbed Romeo as he fought against them. He was able to take two out, but three more men came into the room. They grabbed him as Remus' fist connected with the side of Romeo's face with a crack.

Romeo stared back at him, his gaze filled with rage and contempt. "You chose to side with him. My sister would never abide by that. She has moved on. You need to as well and let her be."

"Oh, your little sister will be mine no matter what, big brother."

"If you harm one little hair on her head, I will kill you."

"Oh? And what about your beautiful mate?"

"I'm already going to kill you for that."

"Ah. I want to see you try. First, you have to find me, and that's going to be hard when you're unconscious."

Remus rammed the butt of his gun into Romeo's temple, and Amanda's scream reverberated off the walls.

She scrambled from the bed and threw on her jeans and shirt. She couldn't find her bra, and her underwear was pretty much shredded. She looked around for a weapon. Suddenly, Remus was in front of her.

"We are leaving," he said as he grabbed her by the arm, painfully.

She kicked and tried to fight him off. Suddenly, she felt a sting across her face and realized he had slapped her. He proceeded to haul her toward the door.

"What about this one?" the guy trying to hold Audri asked.

"Bring her, too. She is a mine."

Amanda looked at Audri, and they both realized they were in deep shit. She looked over to see Romeo in a heap on the floor. Blood pooled all around him, and she hoped that he was still alive with a shiver.

When they were outside, the men slung brown burlap sacks over the girls' heads, and they were thrown in the back of what seemed like a pickup truck. She could smell burning wood around them.

"We will get out of this, Amanda. None of my brothers would let anything happen to us. We have to be strong," Audri whispered.

"I know," Amanda answered. "I am just worried about Romeo."

"Me, too. Me, too. The only two I saw were Bryce and Joseph, and Sebastian had Aurora moving toward the tunnel before that jackass grabbed me," Audri said.

Amanda understood from that moment on that although she was not bubbly like Aurora, Audri would become her friend. She was her family. For the first time in her life, she had a family, and she was determined she was not going to lose it now. She sat quietly and started to think of a plan for them to get out of there.

Amanda laid in a bed that smelled musky and dirty. There were no other furnishings in the room. It was completely bare except a rug in the middle of the floor that looked to be over fifty years old. The dirt caked on it was at least ten years old. Where was Audri?

She sat up and rubbed her hands along her arms and legs. The muscles were sore from being so stiff and in that awkward position in the vehicle. She and Audri had been thrown into the back of an SUV. Their arms were tied behind their backs, and they had gags over their mouths. When they had pulled out of the mountains, the car had pulled over to the side of the road. The girls had looked frantically at each other before everything went black as a bag of some sorts was carelessly thrown over their heads.

She was happy her hands were no longer tied behind her back and that she could rise from the bed. She walked to the only window and pushed back the sheet that someone had nailed in front of it. Her frown returned when she saw that the window had bars placed over it so that there was no way to escape. Unfortunately, all she could see were trees and forest. Wherever they were was high in the mountains. There was no movement outside the window. Everything stood still. She couldn't even hear any birds or crickets.

She turned to walk to the door and tried to open it but screamed in frustration when she saw that it was locked.

Amanda sat back down on the musky bed and waited. Where was Audri? She started to panic a little and then she swung around when the door flung open.

"Remus."

"Ah. So, the beautiful woman has a good memory. Unfortunately, this will probably be an experience that you would rather forget."

"Where is Audri?"

"That little hellion? Oh don't worry; she is fine. Damon would skin me alive if anything ever happened to her." His sneer turned ugly as his beady eyes penetrated through her. It was as if he was thinking of something else entirely. He snapped his head back to look at her. "Good thing Damon is not coming. He might want you for himself, seeing as Romeo killed his mate and all."

"What?"

"Ah. So Mr. Good and Noble hasn't told you everything. Well, I imagine this story he would leave out, seeing as how he is the culprit in the tale."

"I don't believe anything you are saying to me."

"Oh? And why is that? Because I kidnapped you and brought you here?" At her glare, he laughed. "Isn't that the same thing that Romeo did to you? Didn't he keep you prisoner in his little cabin? But you look at me with hatred after sleeping in his bed."

She cast her eyes away from his, knowing that what he said was true. How had she slept with someone she didn't even know? She shook her head, clearing her thoughts. She didn't have time for that right now. She needed to get the hell out of there. This man was nothing like Romeo. He was creepy and made her shudder with dread whenever he was around.

"You are nothing like Romeo. I may not know him personally, but I can tell he is a good person. Something I do not see in you. What do you want with me, and where is Audri?"

"You. Damon is looking at you for the solution to his problem. You see he is without a mate, and since Romeo took his, he plans to return the favor. What he has in store for you completely, I do not know. I just know it is something that you will not enjoy, and Romeo will suffer from it."

"And what do you get out of all this? I know you are not doing it to just help the asshole out."

Amanda cringed inside at the sneer he gave her as his eyes traveled the length of her body. "He promised us a piece of the action." At her look of horror, he laughed and walked up to her. He reached out and roughly pinched her nipple before she could back away. "We will have lots of fun in the next few days. I have told him, however, that I will not take you before the week is out. I will enjoy my time with you for a couple of days before I give you to my men."

She wrenched herself away from him. "You are disgusting and vile. You will not get away with this.

You cannot touch me if I am with child already. And where is Audri?"

His laugh resounded off the walls, giving it an even more eerie sound. "First of all, I don't give a shit about those stupid rules the smaller and weaker communities go by, and second, Audri is fine. Right now, she is in my bedroom, tied to the headboard." He laughed cruelly again.

"You're disgusting." She spit out as far as she could, watching as the driblets of fluid splattered onto his forehead, then started backing away even further when he came toward her.

"We will finish this later." He laughed cruelly as he turned and walked from the cabin. She heard the lock click back into place as he left.

Amanda paced the confines of the small cabin. She needed to get to Audri and help her, but she didn't know how to get out. She looked over at the small fireplace and started planning.

Romeo looked around at the bodies that lay all around the compound. They had pulled together at the end and had defeated the idiots who had attacked. He gingerly touched the back of his head and moaned deep. He knew his head would heal within the day, compliments of being a supernatural, but he wanted the pain gone. His head felt like there were a hundred tiny men inside hammering at the walls with chisels. He looked around and saw Sebastian looking over the bodies.

"What's the count, Sebastian?"

"Thirteen dead and twenty-six wounded. It is not good."

"Audri! Audri! Oh god!" Aurora ran up to them. Her hair and clothes were streaked in blood, and dirt caked her face and hands. Her shirt had been tattered to where her whole midriff was showing and her jeans had a long tear on the right leg. Her feet were bare, and her eyes were wide with fright.

"Audri is gone."

"What!" Sebastian looked out over the bodies, and the three started to frantically search for their sister. After an hour of searching, they decided that she wasn't there at all. "They must have taken her as well. I understand Remus taking Amanda, but why Audri? Payback? It doesn't make any sense."

Romeo looked over at him sadly. "I think there is more to this than that. Something is going on, and I plan on finding out exactly what it is. We need to bury the dead and treat the wounded. Gather as many men as you can. We go after them tonight." He turned and strode back to his home.

"Romeo. There is one more thing." Sebastian looked at him solemnly.

"What more could there be?"

"Benjamin is among the dead. It will be something we will have to tell Audri when she returns. You know she will not take it well."

"That will be something we will face when we get her and Amanda back." Shaking his head sadly, he turned back around and continued on the path to his cabin.

Romeo could sense something was going on; something big. He just wished he knew what it was. Something didn't feel right. He knew Remus was mean and evil and wanted his pack, but there was no way that he would have had enough power to orchestrate everything on his own. No. Someone else was behind this.

Chapter Nine

Audri looked up at the ceiling above her. She was propped up on a stack of pillows, and the bed was facing toward the door. She cringed when it opened and Remus walked through. They had been engaged at one time, before he had turned against the pack and joined forces with evil. She had been so in love with him at one point. He had a gorgeous smile, but it had been corrupted and it showed every time he looked at her. The people he had killed and hurt trying to become the alpha numbered in the hundreds.

"Ah, my sweet, my betrothed, why do you cringe from me? You used to want my touch. You used to beg for it."

"That was before I knew you."

"Ah. I am still the same person. I am just more powerful and stronger than ever before. You should want me more. I have accomplished much since the last time we were together. I can share my power with you now. If we mate, then my magic will join with yours."

"Dark magic! No, I will never mate with you. You disgust me."

"Ah ha! You will not be saying that later on this evening when I join you in my bed. You will be screaming with pleasure, and I will take you over and over. You will mate with me before the end of the week. I will take you every night multiple times until you are so worn and tired that you will agree and mate with me."

"I would rather die. I have someone I have chosen to mate with."

"Who, that snot-nosed kid, Benjamin?"

"He is more man than you will ever be." She glared at him and struggled against the ropes tying her to the bed.

"Ha! You mean *was*, my sweet. I took care of that little obstacle before I came to get you. Sorry about killing your childhood friend, but I couldn't let him take what was mine."

"What! You are lying! You're pathetic. I will never be yours! You hear me, you asshole?" Tears streamed from her eyes, leaving a wet trail to drip from her jaw line.

Remus made his way to the bed and sat on its edge. She tried to scoot as far away from him as she could, but his body just followed, sliding in closer to her. His hand traveled up her arm, and she tried to pull away. When his hand reached the side of her face to gently caress it, she turned her head to the side to try and avoid his touch.

Remus chuckled and gently caressed her cheek. "You belong to me." He leaned down to gently graze her lips with his own. Audri bared her teeth at him and growled, snapping at his lip. He jerked back with a yelp and swiped the pain away. His hand connected with the side of her jaw. He hit her again, and when she refused to acknowledge him, he hit her a third time.

He leaned down into her face and sneered. "You will want me to kiss you later as I take your body over and over." Laughing, he jumped off the bed and made his way to the door. "We will have some more fun later my sweet." He slammed the door behind him.

"Never, you disgusting piece of shit! I will never bend to you. I would rather die!"

Audri stared at the door. She needed to get out of there. Amanda may need her, and there was no way that she was letting that disgusting asshole touch her again. Her hands felt around the headboard for something, and she finally found what she was looking for. A screw stuck out from the headboard. Twisting the rope around the large screw, she ran it back and forth. It was going to take forever to get the ropes to cut this way.

The ropes didn't have any silver in them, and she knew she could Change and rip the ropes apart. The problem with that would be to turn quietly so that she didn't cause any suspicion. She would have to keep from screaming when her bones broke to transform. What many people didn't know was that when a werewolf Changed at any time other than a full moon, it caused excruciating pain. Bones broke and coarse hair grew out from every pore in the body. The ascending of the muzzle was also painful because it stretched the skin and bones in the face.

She worked the screw a little more but made a growling noise with frustration when she realized it wasn't going to work. Taking a deep breath, she started to Change. She turned her head to the side to bite the pillow. Her elbow snapped in the opposite direction, and she gagged on the pillow with the pain. Her other elbow did the same, and then her wrists got larger, turning her hands into paws. It was the most painful, and she muffled her screams.

The hands had more bones than any other part of the body, and each one broke painfully. She was finally able to lift her head and breathe. Her mouth hung open as she took huge gulps of oxygen. She was only half-turned. Knowing she wouldn't be able to turn the rest of the way without making noise, she started turning back into her human form now that she was released from the rope bindings. Using the pillow again, she started the painful process.

Audri laid there for a while, trying to catch her breath, and then stood on shaky feet. Stretching out her arms and legs, she bent over and touched her toes. She stood back up and reached her hands high up to the ceiling. When she once again felt like herself, she started to search the room for some clothing. She found a long button-down shirt and slid it over her nakedness. She made her way to the window and looked out the panes to see nothing but trees and wilderness. She slowly lifted the window to keep from making any noise and peeped her head out to see if there was anyone around.

Upon seeing there was nothing but trees outside the window, she silently eased out of the window to land on her feet. With her back flush against the wall, she eased around to the corner of the building. She peeked her head out to glance quickly to see what lay ahead of her. Seeing movement, she crouched back behind the building. Seeing a tree propped up close, she went to stand beside it. Jumping up and grabbing a branch that was hanging low, she hoisted herself onto the next limb. She scaled the tree like a ladder until she was able to climb up on the roof. The shingles pushed against her stomach as she laid flat.

She peered over the top to see numerous men striding about what looked like a small group of homes. In the middle was a large bonfire, and all the men were packing weapons of different sorts. There were shotguns, rifles, and pistols. One house sat off in the distance a little and a total of four men guarded it. That must be where they were keeping Amanda.

She dropped back down to the ground to slide along the side of the homes. She silently made her way around, keeping out of sight. When she came to the last house, she edged her way back until she came to the edge of the woods. Slipping in between the greenery, she made her way through the trees. She smelled the scent of wood burning and something else. It smelled familiar, but she couldn't quite place it. She came to the back of the cabin and saw that there were bars on the window. Peering inside, she staggered back at what she saw.

She heard yelling and turned to run before she was grabbed from behind. Her arms were twisted around behind her back, and she was propelled toward the cabin. She walked calmly through the doorway and raised her chin to glare into a pair of dark blue eyes much like her own.

"Why are you here? You were not supposed to be." The man turned to her and glared.

"Why don't you ask your lap dog? I knew you were low, Damon, but this is hard to believe, even for you."

"Ha! What do I care what you think?" he sneered at her.

She looked away but not before the pained expression crossed his face. "You used to."

"That was before I grew up. I learned that Romeo is not God; something that the rest of you should learn.

"Do you two know each other?" Amanda asked.

Audri nodded. "Meet my brother, Damon, or the shell of the man he used to be."

Amanda gasped out loud. "But I thought I met all of your family?"

"You met all who are alive." Audri glared at Damon.

"Well, as you can see, I am very much alive."

She shook her head. "No, Damon, you are dead to me, as you are to the rest of the family. You died many years ago when you chose that bitch over family."

His face turned pink as he stepped up to her and bent down to put his face close to her own. "That bitch was my mate."

"No, she wasn't. She was evil."

"He killed her. He killed my only attempt at happiness. Now he thinks that his mate has come along and he will live life happily ever after with her. That, dear little sister, is not going to happen."

"You will not succeed, Damon. Romeo will stop you."

"Ha! No, he won't, but it is good to know where your loyalty lies." He sneered at her. "Even though we all know that he has all of you in his pocket."

"And what of father? He gave you life."

He turned his head away to hide the emotion that came across his face. "He made his bed. Now he must lie in it. It was his decision."

"You didn't give him much of a choice, though, now did you?"

"Whatever. Enough about that. Why are you here?"

"I told you to ask your lap dog. Remus brought me here and told me about how much fun we are going to have."

Damon's face turned red. "Find him now!" he snapped at one of his men.

Remus strutted into the room with his head held high a few minutes later.

"What is the meaning of this, Remus?"

Remus sneered "What do you mean?"

"Why is my sister here?"

Remus turned to see Audri glaring at him with her hands on her hips. "You said I could have what I wanted from the village, just to leave the bitch untouched and that Romeo was yours. I want Audri."

"No! You know she is off limits. You will not take her. She is to go home immediately. Now that she knows everything, Romeo will know who has his mate."

"All the more reason for me to keep her." Remus laughed out loud as he looked up and down Audri's physique.

"You will never touch me, you disgusting jackass. Do you understand me? I would rather die than lay with you. And if you force me, I will never stop trying to kill you." She spat in his direction.

He laughed again. "You may try, my sweet, but that is one thing that will never happen."

"I got out of that little trap you just set for me, didn't I?" She laughed at him, which made him glare even harder at her.

"You will have someone take her home! Now! Do you understand me? If you do not, then I will kill you myself, Remus!" Damon's voice thundered through the house and off the windows, making them shake.

Remus turned to stomp away. Somehow Audri knew this wasn't over. Turning, she glared at Damon. "We thought you were dead. Why didn't you come home? Why are you doing this? You need to let her go."

Damon shook his head. "Why am I doing this? Maybe because he killed my mate. Do we have to keep going over this? He took my mate from me, and now I will take his mate from him. The end! And as far as the family is concerned, I am dead. I died with the one person who accepted me for who I was."

"We accepted you, Damon. We just couldn't accept her. She was evil."

"No, you wouldn't accept her because she was a witch. And look what we have here. Romeo's mate is a witch, too. Seems only fair that I kill her. That is, after I make Romeo suffer like he did me."

"No, Damon. Don't do this."

A huge explosion shook the house, and Damon strode to the door. Looking back at the two men inside, he growled at them, "Stay here. Do not let either of them out of your sight, especially my sister. Got it?" At their nod, he turned and walked out the door.

Audri looked at Amanda and nodded. "Are you alright?'

"Yes, fine. How about you?"

"I'm pissed but okay. We need to find a way out of here. He put those baboons at the door, so that is out. Unless we can sneak past them somehow. Maybe if I cause a diversion, then you could get away."

"Absolutely not, Audri! I am not leaving here without you. There is another way, I'm sure."

The women sat at the table and listened to the ruckus and noise coming from outside. Suddenly, there was a huge splintering sound as the front door was broken in. Remus stood on the threshold. He sneered at Amanda and walked up to her, hitting her hard in the head. She slumped sideways.

"What the fuck are you doing? Get away from her." Audri fought against Remus, although she knew she was no match for him. She flew through the air to land against the wall. She felt a sharp pain on the back of her head and reached up to steady the spinning. When she pulled her hand away, she saw the blood and fainted.

Remus gathered Audri into his arms and strode away from the house. He placed her into the cab of the truck and pulled a rope laced with silver from the glove box. Wrapping first her wrists and then her ankles with it, he laid her in the seat. As he drove from the little group of cabins that had been his home for years, he looked into the rear-view mirror. Smoke billowed into the clouds from the fire consuming the houses. He pushed the gas pedal down when he heard the sound of wolves howling into the morning light. The sun was starting to rise, and he wouldn't have the comfort of the night hiding him for much longer. He knew that Romeo was near and pushed the truck even faster.

Chapter Ten

Romeo saw the smoke clouds up ahead. He could smell his sister and Amanda in the air. He knew they were this way. He knew he had to head toward the smoke. He just worried what he would find when he got there. He turned around and nodded at his brothers and pack. They knew that they had put everything, including their lives, on the line when they went forward. But he knew by their stance that they did it with pride for their king as well as their queen. He and Amanda may not have mated, but they all looked to her as the alpha queen. She didn't know what she was or how to Change, but in time all of her powers would come to her.

The worst part about going forward was not knowing who or what they were up against. Remus was after Audri. What he didn't understand was why he had taken both women. Remus had always been infatuated with Audri and had followed her around everywhere, even though she did all she could to make him go away. But why Amanda?

Mentally and physically shaking his head, he started forward so that he could finally find out what was going on. The smoke was coming from high up in the mountains, and it would take them hours to get there.

They came to a point in the mountain where the air changed and there was a different smell. Something familiar, but he couldn't place where he had smelled it before. Ahead of him, through the trees, he saw men standing with weapons. They were perched in trees and a few were on the ground. These must be the guards. There were a total of five that he could see. He made a motion with his hand, and the other men in the pack took the cue and circled around.

The men were easily subdued when they saw who led the group of werewolves. They watched Romeo with fear as he yelled and bantered at them to find out where the women were. The men knew who Romeo was and knew the effect of his anger. The information that he wanted quickly escaped their lips, and they were bound. Some of the pack stayed behind to watch over the men as the rest of them made their way up the mountain.

Amanda woke to find herself inside the little cabin again. She coughed on the smoke that surrounded her and eased completely against the floor. She slid silently, keeping her head down until she came to the door. She peered through the opening to see nothing but smoke and flames. Her head pounded, and she tried to stand. Suddenly feeling dizzy, she dropped back to her arms and knees. She was jerked back up by her hair.

"Come on, witch. You are going with me." She looked up at Damon and knew that there was no way she would be able to escape from him as long as she was suffering from the concussion. She just looked at him as he grabbed her wrist and started to drag her behind him. She tripped over her feet twice before righting herself and stumbling forward again. He just grumbled in front of her. When they finally reached a large SUV, she leaned her back against it and gulped in large breaths of air.

"Why are you doing this? Because something happened to your mate? You know that I had nothing to do with it. Why make me suffer?"

He looked at her as he would a small child. "I am sorry that you are caught in the crossfire. It was not my intention to make you suffer, just Romeo."

"Damon?"

Amanda turned to see Romeo standing in front of them. He stared at the man holding her forearm with wide eyes.

"Hello, Romeo." Damon sneered at him.

"You are alive! We all thought you were dead. We saw you go over with Elena. What are you doing here? And why didn't you tell us that you lived?"

"I have been planning this day for over a year. I have been waiting to see the torment in your eyes when you lose your mate. I will take everything from you that should have been mine. I was the eldest and what happened? Father made you alpha because he didn't approve of my mate. Well, too bad. Now, I will take your mate, and you will suffer as I have this past year."

"I am sorry about Elena. I really am, Damon. But it was not something that was in my power to stop. She was not right for you. She was cruel and vindictive."

"You will not say her name again. Her sweet name shouldn't come from lips that are corrupted with unjust criticism. She was an angel. My angel! And now she is gone because of you. You took her from me!" Damon's anguished cry echoed across the mountains as he lunged for Romeo.

"No, Damon; she did it to herself. Please brother, stop this."

"You are not my brother. None of you are." Damon swept his hand out to include all of the people around them. "This isn't over." He glared at Romeo.

Before they knew what he was doing, he shoved Amanda toward Romeo and jumped into his truck. The wheels screeched as he raced away in the large SUV, almost hitting two people in the process. The men turned to go after him. Raising his hand, Romeo looked sadly at his pack. He tightened his arms around Amanda. Making sure she was alright was his biggest concern. "Let him go. I will deal with him later. We need to find Audri."

Amanda grabbed two handfuls on his shirt to keep herself as close to him as she could. She had buried her face against his chest as he held her close. She felt safe and warm, and for the first time in her life she felt like she belonged. She raised her head to gaze into his eyes. "Remus took her. They are in a large truck. I could hear the engine, and it was loud."

He nodded and kissed her forehead as he swept her hair back from her forehead and ran his hand down its length. "Are you okay? Did either of them hurt you?"

"Nope, just pissed me off and your sister, too. She escaped to come rescue me. Damon didn't know she was here. He was pissed when he found out and demanded Remus release her, but Remus said no. Next thing I know, I'm waking up in the floor, bleeding, and there's smoke all around me. Then, Damon grabbed me."

"It's okay, honey. Come on; we are going on to look for Audri. We will stop at a hotel so you can rest. I will leave someone with you." She nodded and let him lead her to a truck that suddenly appeared. It was the first time he'd used the sweet name with her, and she felt her heart softening for this man. Remus and Romeo could not be any more different.

Amanda looked up at the large neon sign as they pulled into the parking spot. She glanced at Romeo and smiled. She waited patiently as he went into the small office and returned with a key. He drove around to the other side and parked the truck. He held the door open for her as she stepped inside. It wasn't anything fancy, but there was a large bed and a shower and that made her happy.

"I want a shower."

"Go on. I will get us something to eat."

She walked up to him and instantly his arms wrapped around her waist and brought her against him. "I would rather you join me."

He chuckled into her ear. "I would love nothing more, but we need food. I will be back." She felt the light smack to her ass before he turned to leave. Amanda sighed as she started to undress and make her way to the bathroom. When she was finally standing underneath the spray of water, she put both palms flat against the wall and leaned into it while the water pummeled her back and ass. She was in heaven. She jumped when she heard the shower curtain being pushed to the side. Romeo stepped into the shower in all his nakedness and smiled at her as she straightened.

"I thought you were going to go get something to eat."

"I did. You have been in here a while."

"I was just thinking.'

His hands gripped her hips and brought her closer. She could feel the warmth of his breath against her cheek. "Hmmm. what were you thinking about?" His lips coursed a trail from her ear to the top of her shoulder.

"You, and how my life has changed from this little vacation."

"Hmmm, that it has. Mine as well. But what are you going to do about it?"

"Well, right now, I am going to take advantage of the moment." Her small hands traveled from the top of his shoulders down his sides and back up to grip his biceps. She wrapped her hand around to the back of his neck and brought his head down to capture his lips with hers. His hands gripped her rounded hips tighter and brought her flush against him. He kissed her and backed her into the wall. His hands reached around to grip her ass and bring her so that his member scraped against her most delicate parts. She moaned into his mouth and moved against him, trying to find as much friction as she could. He chuckled into her mouth and finally released her lips.

"We need to get out of this shower. It's getting cold, and your body is starting to look like a prune. Not that I wouldn't like to lick every single one of those creases. Come on." He leaned down and turned the water off. He stepped out of the tub and reached for a towel. She smacked his bare ass and giggled.

He grinned over his shoulder. "Paybacks are a bitch, little one."

"Ha!" She grabbed the towel he held out and ran out of the bathroom. She giggled when he ran after her. She looked at him over the bed and went to move left. He followed her. When she faked and tried to go right, he jumped onto the bed. He finally reached her and pulled her laughing and squealing onto the bed. He pulled both arms over her head and trapped her wrists with one hand. He grinned down at her. She looked up to see a devilish glint in his eye and exhaled the breath she had been holding in. His head dipped down to trace small kisses along her jaw line. She moaned, and he looked down into her aggravated face.

"Why did you stop?"

"Patience, my dear." He licked the inside of her ear and she growled from deep in her throat. He chuckled. "You don't seem to like my game too much."

"If you don't stop playing with me, I'm going to…" Her words drifted off when he leaned down and sucked her nipple into his mouth.

"Hmmm. You're going to what?"

"Please… Damn you, stop teasing me."

He traced her nipple lightly with his finger and then reached down to take it into his mouth again. She moaned loudly again. He chuckled again before he took her mouth with his again. She kissed him back with everything she had. The heat radiated off his body and mingled with her own. She smelled his natural scent; a little of spice and musk, and reveled in it.

His lips traced her face; her eyes, lips, cheeks and nose were touched and cherished with his lips and then his hand. She looked up at him in wonder. Nobody had ever made her feel like he did. She felt special and beautiful. She had changed so much since meeting Romeo. She had never allowed herself to be completely free with anyone, especially when it came to her body. Now, here she was, giving everything she had to this man who had changed her life. For the first time she just felt. She didn't think about the consequences or what was going to happen next or what anyone else thought about it.

"How do we mate?"

"What?" He leaned back from kissing along her collarbone to gaze down at her.

"You heard me. How do we mate?"

"We give ourselves freely and then we must bite each other in climax."

"Do you want that?" She looked up at him.

He swept the hair behind her ear and smiled at her. "More than anything."

"Then let's do it."

"You do understand that this is permanent? You have to be sure. Your body will not respond to any other man as long as I'm alive. You will feel me even when I am not with you. We will communicate without saying a word. You will crave me when we are away from each other for too long, and last, you will go into season in a matter of days, which could release all your other powers. Are you ready for that?"

She brought his head down to hers and kissed him deeply. "First of all, you are the only man that I want to touch me. Second, yes, I am ready. Mate with me tonight."

He couldn't contain the growl that started deep in his throat. "Yes! But be forewarned; this is going to be fast and hard, and there is no stopping it once we start."

"Good. Now take me and stop all this talking."

He chuckled and kissed her deeply. His hands slid down over her stomach and abdomen to slide against the outside of her entrance. He traced her slit and smiled at the deep moan she let out. She no long worried about her weight. She only worried about him and how good he felt against her and how his touch made her desire flame higher than it ever had before. Her hips shifted upward to rock against his hand involuntarily, and she moaned again. He scraped his teeth against a nipple and then sucked it into his mouth. He twined his tongue around the engorged flesh. Her gasp was like music to his ears. His finger reached her opening, and he circled it lightly teasing her with his hands and mouth until she was writhing against the bed, moaning deep in her throat. He slipped a finger inside her and then another, stroking her deeply.

"Please, Romeo. Take me."

He eased his hips between her thighs and stretched them wider apart. He rested the head of his penis against her opening and looked down into her eyes.

He kissed her deeply before releasing her lips and growling as he slowly slid inside her, "You are mine."

"Yes. Please, Romeo, make me yours." His length slid inside her depths, stretching her in delicious wonder. Her eyes met his as he slid in until he was fully seated inside her.

"Yesssss!"

"My god, you are so tight and feel so good. I will never let you go."

"Good!"

He started to move, slowly easing out of her before sliding back in again. He kissed her everywhere his mouth could reach and kept his pace slow and easy.

"Faster, please. Harder, please. God, you are killing me here."

He chuckled but sped up. "I don't know how much longer I can take this."

"Let go, Romeo. It's okay. I am here. I can handle it. Take me." She smiled up at him as she raised her hips to meet his thrusts. Before she knew what he was doing, he lifted her and turned her onto her stomach. She raised herself onto her knees and arched her back, pushing her ass into the air.

His hand landed sharply across her ass. He leaned over her, and she felt his chest against her back. The small sprinkles of hair tickled her. "That was for in the shower." Another smack. "That was because I know you liked the first one."

She moaned deeply as he slid inside her. He didn't let her adjust this time but instead slammed into her over and over. She clenched around him with her climax and he groaned, holding back for her next one. When he thought he couldn't take anymore, he flipped her back over onto her back and leaned over her. Her knees were against her chest as he rammed into her so hard she scooted up the bed.

Finally he growled deep in his throat. "Now! We have to do it now. I can't hold on." His fingers found her clit and circled it. He felt her walls start to tighten around him and leaned over. "Now, baby. Bite me." He gave her his shoulder, and when he felt her teeth elongate and pierce his skin, his mouth clamped onto her shoulder.

Amanda felt her mouth change. Somehow, she had sharp teeth that had pierced Romeo's skin, and she felt the coppery taste of his blood on her tongue. It wasn't gross like she thought it would be. Rather, it had a hint of him, a sweet, spicy flavor with a musky aftertaste. She soared with the revelation of his blood, his warmth. The climax hit her all at once, taking away her breath. She saw stars and felt like she was going to pass out with the extreme intense pleasure that enfolded her.

Romeo tasted her sweetness like berries. It was more than good. It was amazing. She was amazing. He'd never thought it would feel like this. This was extreme pleasure like he had never known. It was more than sex; it was destiny. His and hers, and it was now irreversible. She was his, and no one would ever take her from him.

Chapter Eleven

They both lay beside each other in the bed on their backs, looking up at the ceiling, panting and trying to calm their racing heart rates. He rolled to his side to look at her and smiled. His hand automatically settled on her stomach, and he drew small circles on it. Tracing along her side, he caressed upward until he reached her arm. Sliding up her arm, his finger traced where her mating mark now stood out against her skin. She was now marked for all time as his. Next, she would become his wife and bear his children then no one could ever take her away from him.

She looked up into his eyes and smiled. "You look solemn and worried. Is something wrong?" Alarm quickly clouded her eyes.

"No, sweetheart. I was just thinking that there is no way that anyone could take you away from me now." He smiled down at her then.

"You act like I could be taken before. You would come for me even if we hadn't mated."

"That's true. Know this; I will always find you. No matter where you go. No matter how far. I will find you. You were made for me and nobody else. You will forever be mine; only mine."

Her hand caressed his cheek. "And you mine. I love you. I know it has only been a short time, but I have never felt like this before. I feel stronger and more alive than ever when you are around."

"I do as well, my love. I love you more than you will ever know." His lips teased across hers briefly. When he leaned back up, he smiled at her.

She was suddenly surrounded by a bright white light, like a halo. She turned frightened eyes at him. He reached out his hand right before she vanished completely. Romeo jumped from the bed looking frantically around the room. She was gone. Where did she go? He pulled on his pants and headed to the door. Outside, Sebastian ran to him with wide eyes.

"What happened? There was a bright light coming from your room. Is everything okay?"

"No. She's gone."

"What? Who?"

"Amanda. She's gone. We mated, and then there was a bright light, and then she was gone."

"Come on. There has to be a reason for this. Let's call Dad. He will know what's going on. We can split up. Half of us go in search of Audri and the other half after Amanda."

Romeo nodded and let his brother pull him back into the hotel room. After talking to their father, Sebastian slipped the phone back into his pocket. He looked at Romeo sadly.

"Father thinks she came into her powers. Since she is not aware of how to use them, then we must wait for her to reach out to us. She could be anywhere now."

"Damon."

"No. Neither of us thinks Damon took her this time."

"No. I did this to Damon. What I am feeling now. He felt this, and now I understand his anguish." Romeo felt an emptiness deep in his gut. He had known back when he killed Elena that he would cause his brother emotional pain, but he had never imagined it would be physical as well. It was as if a piece of himself had been ripped apart. He had to find her and make sure she was alright. Then, he needed to find Damon and make things right.

"Any news on Audri?"

"I don't think Remus will harm her. You know as well as I do that he loves her. Always has. Things have just twisted him, then finding out about Benjamin was his undoing. Now that Benjamin is gone, who knows?" Sebastian shrugged his shoulders, but Romeo read the worry in his eyes.

He nodded and started gathering their things. They didn't have time to rest now. As he left the little room, his hand automatically went to the mark on his shoulder, and he vowed that he would find her and bring her home where she belonged.

<<<>>>

Audri looked over at the man she had thought she would spend the rest of her life with at one time. He wasn't the same person he was then. He was different, cruel, now.

"What happened to you?" Something in her needed to know.

"What happened to me? Nothing. I faced reality and found out what you and your family were really all about. I found out what had happened to Damon, and you can say I sympathized with him."

"You used to care about people. You used to care about me, and now it is all about you."

"Well, there was one other person I cared about, but your brother put a stop to that too, didn't he?"

"Elena? You had a thing for Elena? But you were with me."

"Do you really think that I would pass up joining with a witch like her? She was a Radiant and rare, as well as my ticket to immortality."

"That's what this is all about… immortality?"

"Oh, no. I wanted her for her immortality, and I wanted you because I have always wanted you. I followed you around when we were kids, for Pete's sake. You were to be my mate, and then you met that sniveling little pup Benjamin. Suddenly, I wasn't good enough for you anymore. So, now I have taken him out of the equation, and I will finally have what I have wanted since we were kids; you!"

"You could have had me before, but you got mean and evil and joined Damon. Elena was his mate, and you chose to be on their side. You chose against me. This is not my fault, and it definitely wasn't Benjamin's."

"No. I guess not." His shoulders lifted in a careless shrug, and he grinned at her evilly.

Audri saw red at his casual smugness over Benjamin's death. "He was my betrothed, you son of a bitch."

"No! I am and always have been your betrothed. No other will ever take my place, now or after. Do you understand that?"

"Yes. I understand that you are crazy now and always have been. I was just too blind to see it. Now I do, and you will not get away with this. My brothers will stop you."

"Ha! Your brothers are too busy looking for Amanda, the queen. You are just a female wolf to them and everyone else in the pack."

"No. You forget I am royal blood. I am royalty and my pack look up to me, and I am important. It was you who was just another wolf. You were not worthy of me to the pack. Remember that."

"I know one thing. They will be singing a different tune after today. I will take you as my mate and then after the rest of your family has a little accident, we will rule the pack as the last surviving royal bloodline."

"That will never happen."

"We will see, my pet." He stopped at a motel and turned the car off. It was late and dark. Audri looked down at her tied wrists and ankles and knew there was no way to get away. She didn't want to think about what he had planned for the night.

"Don't worry. We will not mate tonight. I may do a little petting and exploration, but I have something planned for our mating ceremony." He gave her a look that traveled the length of her body and back up to her eyes.

She spat toward him. "You make me sick!"

She heard his laughter as he got out of the truck and walked toward the small office. It was pitch black outside, and they were at a little rundown hotel in the middle of nowhere. He had even driven off the highway for thirty minutes before they found the place. He had tied her wrists to the steering wheel, so there was no way that she could even attempt at opening the door. She had to wait until they got in the hotel before she tried to get free. If her brothers didn't come soon, then she was going to have to succumb to Remus' desires in order to get away. That was one thing that she was not looking forward to.

Taking a deep breath, she looked up to the heavens to pray that her brothers would hurry and then turned her attention to the man walking out of the office, grinning and waving a key card in her direction. She cringed inside when she thought about lying next to him all night.

Amanda found herself in a room that was bright and colorful. An attractive man leaned against the wall. He smiled at her and threw her a gown, turning around to give her some privacy.

After she was dressed, she cleared her throat. "Who are you, and where am I?"

"Why, I am Dean; your brother. Or at least half-brother, and right now you are under my charge."

She looked up at him with wide eyes. "What?"

"Sit and I will explain everything."

She made her way to a chair and looked up at him, expectantly.

"What are you talking about, my brother?" Amanda looked at the man like he had grown three heads.

"You see, mom was a regular floozy in her day, it seems. I am two years older than you. Mom was in another marriage before she met your dear old dad. The marriage she should have been in. You shouldn't be here. She tainted our bloodline with dog blood. You are a disgrace to the Wilson line. We are fae; powerful beings that surpass any other in this world or realm. Mother was special. She was what is known as a Radiant. They are always pure blood fae and wield power like you have never known. They are the ones who control all elements on this world. There are four in general alive at a time. These four beings stand for the powers that hold this world together. Earth, wind, fire and water. Mother was an Earth Radiant. We have been searching for many years to find where her powers generated. I thought she would pass them to me, but she didn't. She couldn't have passed them to you, because you are only part fae. Therefore, she must have yet another child out there that we do not know about, or she passed the gift to a fae she knew in passing. I have searched all her close friends. If they had the powers, then they were released when I took care of them."

"You killed them?" At his cold stare, she knew he did. "Over some stupid powers; are you serious? Well, rest assured that I do not have them. As you said, I am not pure blood, and second, I have not had any powers come to me at all."

"Oh, dear little sister, you spent your entire life in the human world and never knew you even had powers. You suppressed them unintentionally and could not be aware of them. Have you ever had any dreams that came true or felt a jolt of deja vu? That was your powers trying to be released, but you wouldn't believe anything was out of the ordinary. Even though you felt it, you brushed it off, and they stayed suppressed. Tsk, tsk, tsk; now, look. You went and slept with a damn dog, and your powers have come to the forefront. Why, look at you. You are simply glowing with the suppressed magic inside you. I didn't think you would be powerful at all, but it looks like I was wrong as well as father. You might actually be of some use to me in the end. Until then, you will stay here while I get rid of those ridiculous dogs that are hounding after you."

"No. Leave them alone." She stood and faced the man who said he was her brother. "You are no brother of mine, and I will not allow you to hurt them." Her eyes started to glow a golden brown color. "You see, dear brother. Romeo is my mate."

"Ahhh. Damon said that you might be stupid enough to mate with him. He had hoped you did to make him suffer. I had hoped you wouldn't. I knew with a mating all your potential would be out in the open." He lifted his hand and a bright light shot its way around her waist and pulled her back against the wall. He shot out two more bright flashes. One wound its way around her wrists to hold them against the wall while the other trapped her ankles. "I thought you might say that. You know, with the whole mating thing and all. This will keep you busy for a while."

He laughed at her as he stepped closer until their noses were almost touching. He sneered down into her face. "You see, everyone thinks that you are going to be powerful. I don't. Actually, I foresee your death in the near future. These bindings will keep you here, and I will then make you do my bidding when I return before I throw you to the guards to enjoy. Even though you are not as shapely as they all like, I am sure they can have a little fun. You may have power, little sister, but you still don't know how to use it, do you?"

She spat at him.

He smashed his fist into the side of her face. She felt a ringing in her ears before a sharp pain radiated from the top of her head to her neck. She had just got cleaned up and recovered from Damon's abuse and now she had to endure this?

"I will see you soon, little sister."

She closed her eyes and listened as he stomped away. When she opened her eyes again, everything was blurry. It took a minute until her vision righted itself. Fifteen minutes later, she still had an agonizing pain radiating from her head.

"You have to look within yourself. You have the power to break the bonds. You are powerful. You just have to believe it." She looked over to where the voice was coming from and saw a woman standing there. She was petite with long blonde hair and a beautiful face.

"Who are you?"

Completely ignoring her question, the woman started talking in that same soft voice. "I do not agree with Dean and the others, but unfortunately, there is nothing I can do about your predicament. I do not have the power to go against a Radiant offspring. Especially one as trained as he is. He has been mastering spells and powers since we found him at age six. He is very powerful, but he is also evil. I see blackness inside him. That is my gift as a fae; to see the soul of others. His is dark and not good. Here, you must be thirsty." She walked to Amanda, and a cup magically appeared in her hand. Although, she shouldn't be surprised after learning of werewolves and such, Amanda gasped.

"How do I know I can trust you? How do I know that you did not poison the water and are working with him?"

"I understand." She bent her head to take a drink of the water and then opened her mouth to show Amanda that there was indeed water in her mouth. She smiled as she swallowed. Even though Amanda knew that the woman could have done some kind of magic to make the water appear in her mouth, she was extremely thirsty and wanted the water.

She took deep, healthy gulps of the water as the woman held it to her lips.

"You are powerful, Amanda. You have much light in your soul and can break the bonds that he has on you. But you must believe in it. You must believe in yourself. When you are true, your powers will be like nothing that has ever been seen. I also see the future, and I will tell you that what you become will be a first for all beings. You are the key to the supernatural existence in this realm. You are our key to happiness and life." She smiled tenderly at Amanda and stepped back away from her. "I must go. If any of the others find out I was here, then I will be severely punished. Just remember what I said. You have the power. Believe in yourself."

"Wait! Who are you? What is your name?"

The woman vanished instantly, and Amanda sat there, huffing with frustration. What in the hell was going on? Was she really some magical being? She didn't have wings; that was for sure. She had heard the word fae in some of the stories she read and knew they were something close to a fairy. The one thing that the Disney characters didn't tell you, however, was that not all fairies were light and happy. Some were dark and evil.

She shook her head. She had already pinched herself multiple times to see if she was dreaming and knew she wasn't. She looked down at the glowing ropes and tried to pull her hand out but the rope just tightened around her wrist even more.

Screaming with frustration, she thought back to her time with Romeo. She had seen for herself that he was a werewolf. Could she truly be a fae? It was a lot to take in, but what did she know? One thing was she really didn't know her parents or about them. Her mother had met her father when she was sixteen. How could she have possibly been married earlier than that? She was just a child.

Amanda needed to find out more about her mother.

Chapter Twelve

Audri woke to find herself in bed with Remus behind her. He was spooning her and had his arm draped over her waist. She tried to sneak away, but his grip tightened.

"Where are you going, my sweet? We were just getting cozy. Didn't you enjoy last night?" His hand left her stomach to capture and fondle a breast in his hand. She had been grateful that all he had done was touch her. He had said that he had their mating planned and it was going to be special, so he didn't want to take her until then.

The loud cracking of a door slamming open made them both jump. She looked up, expecting to see Romeo and her brothers, but instead, Damon stood there.

"I told you that my sister was off limits, you little worm!" Damon bellowed so loud that the window panes rattled. She had known he had power, but not like this. He walked to the bed and pulled Remus up by his shirt front then flung him across the room. "You just don't get it, do you, weasel? I told you no and then you go behind my back. You are no better than they are."

Audri looked at the man who used to be her brother and cringed in fear. His face was blotchy and red with anger, and he bared his teeth at Remus. She had never seen any of her brothers this angry. "Damon. Please calm down. You are going to hurt yourself."

He turned his murderous stare in her direction. "Did he hurt you?" When she shook her head, he went on, "Did you ask to come here with him?"

When she shook her head again, he walked over to pick Remus up and fling him across the room again. This time, the man did not move afterward. His lifeless body slumped from the sink down to the floor. Audri muffled a gasp behind her hand. When Damon started to walk her way, she backed up instinctively. He held his hand out to her, and she saw the sadness in his eyes.

"I would never harm you, Audri. You have to know that." She walked to him and took the hand he offered. He gathered her close, and tears streamed from her eyes as her brother held her in his arms. This man, this protective man, was her brother again. She knew that he was powerful, but she had never seen anything like the force he had used against Remus. He pulled her from his chest and looked at her with a sad smile.

"I am sorry you were in this, Audri. I need to go, and I think you should, too. Nobody saw you with him, and I hear sirens in the distance." Although she could not hear them, she knew that her brother probably could, since he had alpha blood. "Tell father…"

"I will. And Damon; he loves you, too. Come home. It is where you belong. You are family, and we all love you and want you back where you belong." Tears streamed steadily down her cheeks.

"No. I only have a little time left, and I will spend it in solitude. I want to go to the mountains and die happily by myself."

"What do you mean, you only have a little bit of time left?" She looked at him worriedly.

"Black magic has its price, cupcake." He grinned at her when he called her the nickname he had called her when they were kids. She had been cupcake, and he had been called puddin' pie.

She looked up at him with sorrow in her eyes.

He smiled. "It is alright. You have much to look forward to. Benjamin is on his way."

"But Remus said he killed him."

"No. He is very much alive and on his way here to find you. He will make you happy. I have one more favor to ask of you, little sister."

She hated that she was still a little skeptical, but she looked at him warily. "What?"

"Tell Romeo that he needs to look to Amanda's family to find her. Tell him to be wary of her brother."

"Wait, she has a brother?" She looked at him questioningly. "You sound as if you know first-hand."

"I have done some things that I am not proud of. Tell Romeo that he is powerful but his weakness is in his uncle's adopted daughter, Lilith. They have been having an affair, and she is his partner in all things. And Audri, I mean all things evil, including dissolving Amanda's powers."

"I will, Damon, but I wish you would reconsider coming home."

His hand caressed her cheek. "I am sorry, little one, to you and everyone. Please tell Romeo."

She covered his hand with her own. She was too emotional to say anything and could only nod.

Audri watched as he turned away from her, showing her his back. As he walked away without turning back, she tried wiping the tears from her eyes. Unfortunately, they kept running down over her cheeks and disappearing into the top of her shirt. She sniffed when she finally heard the sirens that he had been talking about. Making her way to the door, she stepped outside. At the end of the building, she laid her head against the brick and took numerous deep breaths. When her heart slowed down to a normal pace again, she looked around. Unfortunately, they were out in the middle of nowhere. Her choice was instantly made, and she walked toward the line of trees.

Romeo looked down at the top of Aurora's small head. She had been crying non-stop since Audri had been taken. "We will find her, Aurora. I promise."

"I know you will. And I know she is okay. I can feel it. But you know as well as I do that her mouth gets her into trouble. She has a tendency to talk and act without thinking first. I know we will get her back; I am just scared about what condition she will be in."

"I know, but we have to be strong. I know how you feel." The other siblings didn't know what it was like being a twin, especially when that twin was suddenly gone from your side. Sure, they felt sorrow and were upset, but nothing like a twin did. Romeo thought of his own twin. He and Damon were the only other set of twins in the family. When he had thought his brother had died, it was like a part of him had died as well. He felt a hole in his chest that hadn't been filled until he met Amanda. She made everything better and made him feel whole again. He thought of her now and hoped that she was safe. He had to reach her and soon.

He felt even more anguish, knowing what he had done to his brother and what he had put him through. When Elena had come to the tribe, she had been sweet and kind. Everyone enjoyed her company, and it did not matter that she was not a werewolf. They had accepted her as their queen regardless. Sure, there were some who voiced their thoughts, but it wasn't anything they didn't handle. He remembered how Damon used to dote on her and gave her all that she had wanted. He had been so madly in love with her that time had stood still and nothing else in life mattered to him, including his family.

All that had changed, however, the night Romeo had awoken to hear chanting coming from the barn outside. He had eased from his bed and made his way to the doorway of the barn. As he peered inside, he saw Elena kneeling over something on the floor and candles burning. She was chanting in a foreign language and he had stepped closer to get a better look. When he came up behind her, he saw the markings in white chalk on the ground. He knew instantly that she was practicing magic. Black magic. He wanted no part of it anywhere around his family, including his twin brother.

Damon was technically supposed to be the alpha, having been born two minutes before Romeo. Romeo had never been jealous of him or felt like he had been ripped off. He had been happy for his brother. He had been excited for him becoming the alpha, and he had been in awe of him when he found a mate. He had practiced with his brother every day on the fine arts of fighting and running a pack from their father.

Elena had tried to tell him that the spell had been to bring him to her. She had told him that it was him she had wanted all along and that she could give him anything he desired. She had risen to her feet and walked toward him, lacing her hands behind his neck. She smiled at him right before she kissed him. It was at this moment that his brother had walked in. If Damon hadn't been seeing red with rage, he would have seen that Romeo's hands and arms were at his side. He never returned the kiss, but she tried to grab him closer.

They had argued that night and, for the first time, they hit each other out of anger. Damon and Elena disappeared that night, and they didn't see them for a few days. Elena showed back up when Romeo called her. He knew that he had to trick her in order to save his brother. He called her and told her to meet him in a secluded area of the park. When she came, he had taken her into his arms and caressed her body.

The small knife slid down his jacket sleeve into his hand. Her blood-curdling scream rent the air as the blade embedded into her heart. He stepped back, only to be pushed to the side by Damon. As he held her in his arms, she told him things that would haunt him and Romeo for the rest of their lives. She told him how she had wanted Romeo, not him. She had told him how weak he was and how she couldn't depend on him.

Then she lifted the dagger out of her chest and drove it into Damon's. They had disappeared and were never seen again. Everyone thought that the two of them had gone off to die together somewhere, but it seemed that Damon had spent his time healing and planning his revenge. Romeo wished there was some way he could go back to that day. He thought maybe if he had done things differently… His brother was here now though, and it was as if God was giving them a second chance. He was not going to turn it down.

It had been days since Amanda was brought to the house. The young woman came frequently at night when the house was still and silent. She met the rest of her family during those few days as they came to visit her. They all hated her, except for the mystery woman. Her uncle was the vilest. He had married her mother's sister and then her aunt had mysteriously vanished.

The mystery woman wouldn't talk about Amanda's aunt, and she knew that her aunt must have been someone special to her, for there was always sadness in her eyes whenever Amanda said her name. Her uncle and brother apparently had great powers and her adopted cousin was thought to be a Radiant, although she never came into her powers.

Their thoughts were to somehow remove the powers that had suddenly appeared in Amanda and combine them with their own. Their goal was to find out who her mother had given her Radiant powers to. They had tried every spell imaginable but couldn't place who it was. Amanda was their pawn. They would drain her powers and use them to locate the Radiant. She found out from Dean's rambling that Damon had helped them find her. It was his ultimate revenge on Romeo. Dean and his family would drain her of all her supernatural powers in the end, killing her slowly.

"Amanda? It's me. I have brought you fruit and a special gift." She turned to see the petite blonde who she now knew as Penelope.

"Penelope. I am so glad you are here. I must find a way from this room. How do you get in?" There were bars on the windows and the door was locked so there was no way inside the room.

"I use my magic. You can do it, too. You have to believe, Amanda. Here, let me show you this. It may help. I have been searching for it since your arrival. You must read this. It will make things clear. But you must never allow Dean and my father to know of it."

"You are my cousin? No wonder you never wanted to speak of my aunt. She is your mother."

The young girl turned away, but not before she saw the tears well into her eyes.

"Yes. I am your cousin. On the subject of my mother, it is still very hard for me to talk about it. You see, Amanda, my mother was murdered. I cannot prove it, but I know it in my heart to be true. One of these days, I will complete the spell and speak to the other side. Someone killed her for her powers as well." She looked up to meet Amanda's eyes.

"Your father! But how do you know?"

"I know. She was powerful, too. She was a Radiant as well. She was a Wind Radiant. Her powers were given to me. I, however, do not ever use them, for I know my father would kill me for them. That is why I hide; always in the shadows."

"Oh my goodness, Penelope, that is no way to live. You must leave with me now."

She shook her head sadly. "Unfortunately, I cannot. There are others within these walls who need me here. They depend on me to keep things right and make sure my father doesn't go crazy on everyone within the grounds. It is okay. I have come to terms with my life, and I am happy with it. One day, my father will not be here, and I will be free to live. You must know about yourself, though. That is why we are here now. Please read."

She brought the book to her, and Amanda began to read the story. At certain times, she would raise her head and look at Penelope with worry and surprise. When she shut the book, she looked at Penelope with wonder.

"She gave it to me. I am a Radiant. She put a spell on my powers so that I would not know about them or use them until I fell in love. That was what happened with the mating. I acknowledged my feelings for Romeo and the light."

"Oh, no, they come. Here, I will return in a little bit," Penelope said suddenly.

"But, how do I use my power? How do I know what to do?" Amanda was frantic now and worried.

Penelope smiled at her kindly and squeezed her hand. "You have to believe. Believe in yourself, and the power, and then you will know what to do. It will come naturally to you."

The door was pushed aside just as Penelope disappeared with her mother's journal. Amanda looked up to see not only her brother but her uncle as well as his adopted daughter Lilith.

"It seems your dogs are getting closer. I don't want to fight with them right now, so we are going to do the ceremony. Lilith, come forward so that you can harness her powers."

The men went to stand on either side of her. Lilith stood in front of her with an evil smile. Amanda closed her eyes. She had to believe.

There was a bright white light, and she saw the shock on all their faces as the ground beneath their feet began to rise, putting barriers of earth between her and them.

"It's her! She's the Radiant," Lilith screamed. Frantic now, and fearing for her life, she ran to the door.

"How? You are not pure blood!" Her uncle's rage consumed him as his face turned red and he tried to get to her.

"Stay away from me!"

"You dumb bitch. It should have been me. She should have given me the power, not you!" Her brother was shrieking and looked like a three-year-old jumping up and down with a temper tantrum.

Just then, she felt a presence beside her, and she looked to smile into Penelope's face.

"Penelope, why are you here? This is not your place." Amanda watched her uncle try to make his way to them again. But he was held back by a strong gust of wind. "No. You couldn't have. You are Radiant as well?" His eyes rounded with recognition. "Now, I understand. I thought your mother had never given her gift away, and it was trapped here with her spirit, but she did give it away. To you! You little bitch, you never said anything and not once did you use your powers. You will pay for this. I want those powers so I can rule all the fae. I will show you what happens to disobedient little girls, just as I showed your mother."

Penelope's eyes turned completely white as she picked her father up.

"No stop! I'm your father. You can't kill me." His eyes were wide with fright.

"You are no father of mine. Now I will show you what happens to disobedient spouses. You think I didn't know. You think you could keep your affair with your little tramp away from me and my mother. We have more power in our little pinky than the both of you have combined. You didn't want my mother's powers to rule. You wanted them for your little whore. She wanted more and more and you just had to give it to her. Well, no more. This is for my mother."

His scream could be heard as he was thrown from wall to wall and then there was silence. Protruding from the wall was a sharp point from the sconce. Unfortunately, for her uncle, it had found a resting place during all the shaking and commotion. It protruded from his chest, bloody and messy.

He gasped for air as blood trickled from the corner of his mouth. When he took his last breath, Amanda looked around, but nobody was there. Everyone was gone, and she was suddenly alone, as she had always been. The only difference was she had a home to return to and a mate. She quickly made her way outside and began running toward town.

A sharp howl rent the air, and she knew he was with her.

If you enjoyed this title, I would appreciate your leaving a review of the book. Good reviews encourage an author to write as well as help books to sell. Good reviews can be just a few short sentences describing what you liked about the book without having a spoiler. If you could spend 30 seconds writing a review, I would appreciate it: you can review this title right now at your favorite retailer.

Here is a preview of the **next story** you may enjoy:

Romeo Alpha: A BBW Paranormal Shifter Romance - Book 2

"I AM coming, my love." Amanda could hear Romeo, even though he wasn't with her. She realized that they had connected telepathically, just like he said they would, and smiled as she spoke back to him in her mind.

"I know. I am fine." She needed him to believe she was okay; even if she wasn't. She wanted to make sure he was at ease.

"I told you; no matter where you go, I will find you. I will come for you." His voice reached her ears as if he were standing in front of her, talking.

"I am coming to you."

"No, my love. I am here already."

She turned when she heard his voice. Romeo stood before her, in the middle of the field. She hadn't realized how far she had actually run. Her steps quickened the closer she got to him. He gathered her close in his arms and chuckled when she started ripping his clothes from him. He kissed her deeply and pulled her into the circle of his arms.

"We are outside, honey. Anyone could see."

"Come on, aren't you a wolf? Besides, Romeo, don't you think it is time to be ourselves?"

"You make a valid point," he said, in between kisses on her throat.

"Good, then, come on. Let's become one with nature."

He chuckled as he slowly made love to his mate there among the wild flowers and fields.

Amanda knew her work wasn't over. Somewhere out there, her brother was coming up with another plan to take her powers, but for the moment, she wanted nothing more than to feel her mate.

As Romeo slid inside her, she moaned deeply. She didn't need any foreplay or fondling. She just needed him inside her as soon as possible.

He flipped her to her hands and knees and slid inside over and over, speeding up until he was taking her with such force that she lost her balance multiple times. She reveled in it, and met him thrust for thrust, until they both screamed in pleasure.

As they lay in each other's arms afterward, they planned their next step in life and as a couple. They planned their eternity together.

It had been a month since the fiasco of Amanda's kidnapping. Amanda had decided to move into her aunt's estate with Romeo, and they were to be formally married in just two weeks' time. Her powers were growing, and she was grateful for Penelope, who came and helped her to control them. Penelope, Audri and Aurora were like the sisters she had never had, and she found herself becoming very close with them all.

Amanda began to notice that Penelope acted a little strange whenever they came around Elijah, though. Being the quiet one, he often stood aloof when the family was together. He was also the polite one and the one that they all agreed to be the most loyal and family-oriented.

He didn't say much, but his eyes would scan the room for Penelope often. When Penelope also noticed this, her cheeks would turn a light shade of pink. She would often avert her eyes, but Amanda saw the few instances where her eyes would meet his. There was a current of electricity in the air. Amanda could feel the effects of it from across the room. Was that what she and Romeo seemed like to others?

Amanda's brother had disappeared along with Lilith, but Amanda knew that it wasn't over. She could feel her brother breathing down her back. She would catch herself looking around, feeling like someone was watching her. Whether he was close enough to see her or he used his magic, she knew her brother was watching. She had often spoken to Penelope about it, and the other woman had decided to increase the frequency of Amanda's magic lessons because of it.

She guessed the other woman could feel the anxiety building as well. Something was going to happen, and it was going to be big. She knew her brother would have something to do with it, would probably be the whole reason behind whatever chaos would ensue. The only problem was they didn't know what exactly to expect from him. He was sneaky and conniving.

Amanda and Penelope were Radiants; two out of the four most powerful witches in the world. Soon, the news would be out, and the other two Radiants would meet up with them. They were sure of it. Amanda was so excited to meet the Fire Radiant and the Water Radiant.

She was sitting alone on the porch when Penelope made her way over. Penelope was petite and one of the most stunningly beautiful people Amanda had ever seen. She seemed so regal in her posture and movements. But she never seemed to hold herself above others.

Amanda had seen her in the dirt playing marbles with some of the kids just the day before. Her white shirt had been brown by the time she stood up. The funniest part was watching her play the childhood game as her tongue stuck from the corner of her mouth. She had an amazing laugh. Her cheeks had been tinged pink, and her long blond hair had been matted at the ends where it trailed the dirt while she crawled around on her knees.

Penelope had relayed to Amanda the nature of her childhood, or lack thereof. Her father had never allowed Penelope to play with other children, and she often wasn't allowed outside. In the beginning, her mother would sneak her out or she would fight with Penelope's father until he would finally give in and let her go out. Her mother very rarely lost an argument with anyone, including her father. Penelope thought it was in part because he was so scared of her. That was the reason for the poison he'd used to kill her. What a coward.

The servants had told Penelope what happened. They had said her father wanted to take her mother breakfast in bed, and he had them prepare the meal. They figured he must have added the poison on his way up the stairs, because her mother was gone the very next day. Their suspicions about the circumstances grew when he always seemed to be with Penelope's adopted sister, who was just a few years older than herself. She was proved correct when she snuck downstairs in the middle of the night. Lilith leaned over a desk with her father behind her. It was an image that was scalded into Penelope's brain. The worst part was the conversation afterward, where the both of them had clarified their plot to kill her mother.

Two of the servants loyal to her mother were standing in the doorway across from her. One of them had grabbed her and covered her mouth as they took her through a hidden doorway back to her room. They had shushed her and stroked her hair. They had tried reassuring her everything would be okay. They told her that they would help to protect her, and they wouldn't let anything happen to her. That was the last time she ever saw them. A new housekeeper and butler started the very next day. From that point on, she had stayed hidden from everyone, especially her father and Lilith. She knew that her mother had given her powers to her, and she studied on how to use them, but never had the nerve to try anything out.

"Hey, Penelope. What's going on?"

"I came to talk. I wanted to talk to you before, but we needed to be alone."

"Okay." Amanda instantly began to feel worried. What did Penelope not want to say in front of the others?

"Well, you know there are two other Radiants, and we will probably be meeting them anytime now."

"Yes. It is exciting to meet new people, especially ones who will have the same powers as we do."

"Yes, but I don't think you know the full extent of your situation."

"What do you mean?"

"Your power is on the line, Amanda." Penelope looked sad for a moment.

"Well, I mean, I know that. Look, I know I have just recently found out that all of this stuff is even real, and I am just now coming into my full blown powers, but I can learn fast." Would they take her powers from her? Could they do that? She knew black magic could, but would the other Radiants resort to that?

"That is not what I am talking about, Amanda."

"Then what are you talking about?" A chill ran down Amanda's spine. Were there more stories; more secrets?

If you enjoyed this sample then look for **Romeo Alpha: A BBW Paranormal Shifter Romance - Book 2.**

Here is a preview of **another story** you may enjoy:

The Awakening: The Daemon Paranormal Romance Chronicles, Book 1

THE LAST customer of the day was slowly leaving. Phoebe reached down to pet her dog, Ace, and moved to close up shop. Since graduating high school, she had worked in fairs across the country as a fortune teller, saving money. She did not know why, but when she touched somebody's hand, she could read their thoughts. Although she could not divine their future, she could make educated guesses that were enough to bring customers back. After saving enough money, she had finally opened up her own shop.

Removing the scarf from around her hair, Phoebe let her red curls cascade along her shoulders. Ace sniffed at some of his dog food while she reached over to grab her purse. Before she could close up, a knock at the door surprised her. In front of the door, she saw one of the most gorgeous men she had ever laid eyes on. Curious, she opened the door and let him in.

"Hello! How can I help you, Mr...?" She paused and waited for him to respond.

"My name is Apollo Mikos. Pleasure to meet you, Phoebe Williams." The blonde-haired man reached for her hand and shook it. Instantly, a vision arose before her eyes of Apollo and her rolling around in bed sheets. Waves crashed outside the window—a storm was brewing. As the vision of Apollo entered her body forcefully, Phoebe pulled her hand back. The vision went away, but it left a slight blush on Phoebe's cheeks. Reading the minds of other people was occasionally embarrassing and often felt like a major invasion of privacy. Still, she found herself wishing that she could have held his hand a little longer to see where these thoughts took her.

Motioning toward the table and chairs reserved for clients, she asked if he wanted to sit down. Apollo just shook his head.

"I need your help with something, but not like that." He shrugged his shoulders. Tall and well-built, Apollo had blue eyes and chiseled features. He wore a dark black suit that made all of his muscles ripple beneath the fabric.

Confused, Phoebe looked over at him. "What do you mean?"

Sighing, Apollo looked into her eyes. "You will probably want to sit down for this." Still uncertain, Phoebe sat down and waited for him to speak again.

Gazing out the window, Apollo framed his thoughts. "I know your mother, Rhea. I also know what you really are and I need your help."

Phoebe was aghast. "What do you mean? I don't have a mother. I grew up in foster care after my mother left me there when I was two."

If you enjoyed this sample then look for **The Awakening: The Daemon Paranormal Romance Chronicles, Book 1**.

Here is a preview of **another story** you may also enjoy:

Devil's Advocate: A BBW MC New Adult Romance Series - Book 1 by Carla Coxwell

KRISTIE LOOKED at the sky as she pulled up in front of the casino. The air was chilly and the clouds were dark and threatening snow, which was the last thing Kristie felt like dealing with. She had been in her car for over ten hours, driving home from college for the holidays. Her back was sore and her legs needed to be stretched out. She wanted a hot bath in a Jacuzzi tub. She'd settle for a hot tub. But who was she kidding? There was no hot tub to be found at her parents' house and trying to have a hot bath without being interrupted was almost impossible.

Kristie had approached the holidays with an ever-growing sense of dread. It wasn't that she didn't want to see her mother, but every time she came home, it was like being suffocated. Her hometown had held more appeal for her when she was younger, back when her father was alive. Since he'd died and her mother had gotten remarried last year, Kristie had delayed going home at all. She had only met her step-father in passing and hadn't met his nephew, who he tried to raise on his own.

Kristie had saved up to stay at a hotel the entire break. It had made the most sense to her. It would cause the least amount of stress during her stay and give her space when she needed it. But when she had mentioned this to her mother, there was no way to mistake the sadness in her mother's voice for anything else. Knowing she was upsetting her mother by refusing to stay at home with her new family, Kristie had cancelled the reservation and agreed to stay at her mother's house instead.

She looked up at the casino where her mother had worked the last five years. Her mother worked in the back offices, far away from the lights from the slot machines and the sounds of people winning money. The casino was a little run down but brought in a steady stream of people who could afford the middle-level slots and risks it provided in a town that was mostly quiet.

The stale smell of cigarettes and alcohol hit Kristie in the face as she stepped inside. She looked around, seeing if anything had changed since the last time she had been here. Nothing jumped out of her. A few of the slots seemed to have been upgraded, but the carpet was still worn down and dirty and the place had an air of despair that made Kristie's skin crawl. She had never been to Las Vegas, but she imagined that the casinos there weren't as depressing.

Kristie made her way to the back and asked for her mother through the grate where an attendant was standing, looking at her cellphone. The woman went off to find her mother, and Kristie was soon ushered into the back offices. The casino décor quickly ended back here. Her mother's small office was near the back, shoved in a corner. The door was ajar, and Kristie peeked her head in.

Her mother was looking at the computer, squinting through her glasses to whatever was on the screen. When Kristie knocked on the door gently, her mother looked up and smiled. Kristie was startled to see she was going gray. The last time she had seen her mother, she had been a brunette. It was odd to see age creeping up on her. She came over to her and hugged her tightly.

"It's so nice to see you again."

"You, too, Mom."

Her mom urged her to sit down as she sat across from her at her desk. It made Kristie feel odd, as if she was interviewing to be her mother's daughter. Her mom didn't seem to notice, however, and smiled again. They made small talk for a while, mostly talking about Kristie's experiences at college. Kristie felt tired. She knew her mom meant well, but she really wanted to go home and nap. She was only here to get the address to her mom's new place.

"How are things with Lionel?" Kristie finally asked, feeling as if she didn't bring up her mom's new husband, she would never get out of the tiny office.

Her mom seemed to relax now that Kristie had brought him up, "He's great. Really, we're just wonderful. There are some issues, though…"

"Like what?"

"Well, it's actually one of the reasons that we wanted you to stay with us instead of a hotel. See, Lionel's nephew, Gray, is a bit of a handful. Lionel still feels responsible for him since he became his legal guardian when Gray was just a little boy."

Kristie wasn't following, "Okay…"

"He tends to run on the wrong side of the law, and we thought it'd be so great if you two could meet and maybe hang out."

The words hung in the air. Kristie felt a twinge of annoyance. She had thought her mother wanted her at the house because she had missed her, not because she wanted her to play nice with her new step-father's nephew. They weren't in grade school anymore. Trying to change someone set in their ways by sticking them with a goody-goody was a useless attempt.

Kristie took a deep breath and held it for a few seconds, letting the air out slowly. Her mother watched, a worried expression on her face.

"What do you want me to do with him?" Kristie finally asked.

Her mom, taking the fact that Kristie hadn't said no as a good sign, started to ramble. "Well, maybe just hang out with him. Show him what you do for fun. Maybe you two can go to the movies or something."

Kristie raised an eyebrow, "Go to the movies? What does this guy do for fun anyway that has you two so stressed out?"

Her mom avoided her stare and sighed, looking tired. "He runs with a bad crowd and doesn't like to listen. He's a good kid though. He's just lost."

"And you think I can fix him?"

"It wouldn't hurt to try, would it, Kristie? For me?"

Kristie sighed and nodded in agreement. How could she say no to her mother? She would always wish that her mother hadn't gotten remarried, but she didn't want her mom to be unhappy either. Her mom got up and walked over to her, hugging her tightly. Her mother's hugs had always reminded Kristie of being a little kid, outside playing till the sun set and running back inside for dinner. Back when her father was alive. Kristie shut her eyes tightly, willing the memories to leave her. She didn't want to think about her father right now.

Her mom finally pulled away and looked at her, smiling, "We'll have to really talk, you know, all about college and everything."

"Yeah, of course."

Her mom's eyes swept down her quickly, so fast that if Kristie wasn't used to it, she never would have picked up on it. She steeled herself.

"Maybe you and Gray can go to the gym. It'd get him out of the house and you could lose a few pounds at the same time," her mom said cheerfully.

Kristie mumbled in agreement and gave her mother one last hug before leaving the office. She should have known that there wasn't going to be any way in hell that her mother would have let an entire conversation go without making some sort of remark to her about her weight.

As she trudged through the casino, her mood lowered with every step. She regretted coming here for the holidays. Before her, they spread out in a bleak landscape. Dealing with her mother's 'helpful advice' in regards to her weight, and trying to show her loser relative by marriage around town. At the very least, she should have kept the hotel reservation.

Kristie dragged out the drive toward Lionel's house. Her mother had given her the address and it was close to the casino. A ten-minute drive didn't seem like enough time to prepare for whatever she was going to walk into. As she turned down the street where her mom's new house was, she found herself taking a deep breath. The first time, she just drove past the house. It was non-descript and had nothing of worth showing that made Kristie even notice it. Her mom had stopped gardening after her father died, and the front yard of this house was plain and dull.

Kristie pulled into the driveway. The garage door was open and a man was underneath a truck, working on it. She could only see his feet. Kristie got out of her car, grabbing her bags, and looked inside the garage. The man didn't look up when she shut the door of her car.

"Hello?" Kristie called out toward the man under the truck.

He didn't answer. Heavy metal was blasting out of a stereo nearby, but it was such an old stereo that the music sounded tinny. Kristie called out again, but the man still didn't answer. She knew that he heard her because he stopped working at one point and went still before resuming. She hoped this wasn't Lionel, because the guy was an asshole. *Probably his fantastic nephew.*

Kristie trudged toward the front door, leaving the other guy behind. What a fantastic trip this was going to be.

If you enjoyed this sample then look for **Devil's Advocate: A BBW MC New Adult Romance Series - Book 1 by Carla Coxwell**.

Other Books by Darla Dunbar

- Romeo Alpha Blood Lines Romance Series (This series follows "The Romeo Alpha BBW Paranormal Shifter Romance Series")

- The Alpha Feud BBW Paranormal Shifter Romance Series

- The Alpha Packed BBW Paranormal Shifter Romance Series

- The Daemon Paranormal Romance Chronicles

- The Mind Talker Paranormal Romance Series

- The Leather Satchel Paranormal Romance Series

Get the latest update on new releases from the author at:

https://darladunbar.com/newsletter/

About the Author - Darla Dunbar

Darla has been interested in paranormal romance since she was a teenager in high school. It was then that she discovered she could fulfill her fantasies through her writing.

Observing people and human behavior in the area of romance has always been one of her favorite pastimes. Combining that with an overactive imagination is a sure fire way of coming up with interesting themes.

Connect with Darla Dunbar

I really appreciate you reading my book! Here are my social media coordinates:

Friend me on Facebook:
https://www.facebook.com/darladunbar/

Follow me on Twitter: https://twitter.com/DarlDunbar

Check me out on Goodreads:
https://www.goodreads.com/author/show/8425857.Darl a_Dunbar

Subscribe to my newsletter:
https://darladunbar.com/newsletter/

Visit my website: https://darladunbar.com/